POOL OF DARKNESS

At a friend's wedding, Jen falls deeply in love with Alan Littlewood; but their happiness is shadowed by the unexplained death of Lisa, the wife of Alan's brother Graham. In their new village, Jen volunteers to organise an outing to Sellybrook, Alan's historic family home, where she learns the sinister significance of the pool waiting within the willows. Will Jen save or destroy her relationship — and even herself — as she discovers the truth of the Littlewood family's dark secrets?

ANNE HEWLAND

POOL OF DARKNESS

Complete and Unabridged

LINFORD
Leicester

First published in Great Britain in 2013

First Linford Edition
published 2015

C460198524

A catalogue record for this book is available
from the British Library.

ISBN 978–1–4448–2297–7

Published by
F. A. Thorpe (Publishing)
Anstey, Leicestershire

Set by Words & Graphics Ltd.
Anstey, Leicestershire
Printed and bound in Great Britain by
T. J. International Ltd., Padstow, Cornwall

This book is printed on acid-free paper

SPECIAL MESSAGE TO READERS

THE ULVERSCROFT FOUNDATION
(registered UK charity number 264873)

was established in 1972 to provide funds for research, diagnosis and treatment of eye diseases.
Examples of major projects funded by the Ulverscroft Foundation are:-

- The Children's Eye Unit at Moorfields Eye Hospital, London
- The Ulverscroft Children's Eye Unit at Great Ormond Street Hospital for Sick Children
- Funding research into eye diseases and treatment at the Department of Ophthalmology, University of Leicester
- The Ulverscroft Vision Research Group, Institute of Child Health
- Twin operating theatres at the Western Ophthalmic Hospital, London
- The Chair of Ophthalmology at the Royal Australian College of Ophthalmologists

You can help further the work of the Foundation by making a donation or leaving a legacy.
Every contribution is gratefully received. If you would like to help support the Foundation or require further information, please contact:

THE ULVERSCROFT FOUNDATION
The Green, Bradgate Road, Anstey
Leicester LE7 7FU, England
Tel: (0116) 236 4325

website: www.foundation.ulverscroft.com

DANCE OF DANGER

Evelyn Orange

Injured ballet dancer Sonia returns to her family home, Alderburn Hall, to discover that her cousin Juliette is dead. Clues point to Lewis, Juliette's widower, being responsible — yet Sonia still finds herself falling in love with him ... Several mysterious 'accidents' threaten not only her, but also Lewis's small daughter. Is Sonia in true danger? Can she discover the culprit? And can she and Lewis ever count on a future together?

THE UNFORGIVING HEART

Susan Udy

When wealthy businessman Luke Rivers asks Alex Harvey to utilise her specialist skills and decorate parts of his newly purchased home, she is determined to refuse. For this is the man who was responsible for practically destroying her family, something she can never forgive — or forget. Events, however, conspire against her in the shape of her demanding and increasingly rebellious younger brother Ricky and, despite her every instinct warning against it, she finds exactly what Luke Rivers wants . . .

1

Death or life? The dark ripples are offering a choice. She may jump and she may not. Leaving the house, she had been certain she would come here only to gather strength against the coming loneliness. But the pool has its own messages and how pleasant, she thinks, to sink down into the peaceful water. All over. No more betrayals of trust.

Behind her, a reflection moves. Frank, she thinks, her heart jumping. I'm seeing things now. Going back to the happy times. But that's good, isn't it?

Perhaps she has learned to forgive after all. She smiles down to where the movement has been and gone. The first time she has smiled, really smiled, in days — weeks even. Yes, she can move on. She can face up to this new stage in her life and accept the new challenges.

She can step back, away from the edge and onto the path.

The reflection jerks into action and the fist between her shoulder blades is hard and fast. Her feet slide on the damp stones. She screams as she hits the water, with the cold stinging her hands and face like steel. Someone is there, above her, a dark shape against the sun. Surfacing, she gasps, 'Help me.' The dark figure leans over her and pushes her shoulders down, and now her head.

He says, as if speaking to a child, 'But this is what you want. I am helping you. It's easy.'

* * *

Blue flashing lights, strips of blue and white tape blocking the road across the stone bridge. The silver-coloured car in front of Jen's stopped. She sighed in frustration. There must have been an accident or something, and she was already late.

The driver was getting out and talking to one of the policemen. Dark suit, carnation in his buttonhole, strong but expressive face and a great many hand movements. Smiling all the time. You never knew, he might talk his way through.

To her left before the bridge, the ground dropped away from the tarmac with a steep track leading down into trees. Far below, she could hear water beating against rock. Up here there was sun on the grass, but what lay below, out of sight? The other driver was coming towards her now, still smiling but shaking his head; walking with energy and self-confidence. Not really her type. Not if you counted Jim as her type. But Jim was history, forget Jim. She wound her window down.

He said, 'The road will be shut for some time, I'm afraid. Someone jumped off the bridge.' His voice was quick and warm. 'Are you going to the wedding too?'

A moment of sorrow for that

3

unknown person's desperation. 'Yes. The wrapping paper's a bit of a giveaway, isn't it?' She nodded to the gift on the passenger seat, thinking quickly. 'We'll have to reverse back to the main road and go round.' She wouldn't be too late, hopefully, although Lisa would be fuming. Let her fume — but no, that wouldn't be fair on Pamela and it was Pamela's wedding.

'I'll follow you then. Saves me having to negotiate with my sat-nav.'

Jen pushed the gear lever into reverse and shot backwards. Her skin was tingling with heat. Surely not. She couldn't become attracted to someone so swiftly and mindlessly. That went with being fifteen, not thirty-two.

He was driving just a little too close now. She flicked her brake pedal and he dropped back. She spotted the turn and made sure he was indicating too. And now the church was straight ahead and she could leave him to himself while she struggled to find a parking space. No sign of him as she mounted the steps; he must have gone in — but the bride hadn't arrived yet either, so that was all right. She scanned the pews on the bride's side of the church. Where was Lisa? She couldn't see her. Probably she was organising something. She had obviously had a big hand in sending the invitations. Well, Jen had looked. She slid into a seat.

Jen knew this invite had been Lisa's doing. The three of them had been inseparable at uni but after that Jen had let things slide, deciding that she was tired of being organised. Any meetings since had been suggested by Lisa. Jen had made an excuse the last couple of times. But obviously Pamela hadn't minded — or not known how to avoid it. The invitation had even come with a covering note in Lisa's black, confident scrawl: poor Pamela, let's hope it's happiness at last. I think she needs our support, don't you?

But underneath, almost as an after-thought, there had been a spider trail along the bottom. 'Please come, Jen. I need to talk to you.' Not like Lisa at all. This had to be a first. A compliment even, if Lisa actually needed her advice.

Lisa would find her soon enough, no question about that. And as Jen left the church, the tall man was just in front. Yes, Jen thought. A brilliant opportunity to get talking to him. She could make a comment about getting here on time. But she wasn't quite fast enough. Now he was talking to another man, of about the same height but not as thin. A brother maybe? They looked alike. And something about their expressions held her back. She could wait.

There was nobody here she knew. She began to look for Lisa more seriously and knew at last that she wasn't here. Odd, that. She spoke to a radiant Pamela, was introduced to the unremarkable husband and made way for other guests. Now at a loose end, she edged back towards her chance acquaintance, who was still deep in this solemn conversation. Not the right time.

She wasn't intending to listen but couldn't avoid hearing what they were saying. Although she wasn't paying much attention apart from thinking maybe she should give up on this and try making conversation with other guests. Not until the other one said, 'No, not this time. Lisa's left me, Alan. It's finished.'

Jen jerked in surprise. Lisa? This must be Lisa's husband, obviously. What was his name? Oh, yes. Lisa and Graham. She had avoided Lisa's wedding somehow and so had never met him. Not purposely avoided it, she remembered; she'd had flu. But she didn't think Lisa had ever quite believed her. She hovered beside the two brothers, pretending to search for the box of confetti in her handbag. And now she was listening, avidly.

'Left you? When was this? I'd no idea. I didn't know there was anything wrong.'

Graham shrugged. 'You wouldn't, would you? A long time since we last saw you.'

Alan made a swift, dismissive movement of the hands. 'You know Lisa and I never got on.'

'Neither did Lisa and I. Or so it seems, according to her. I hadn't realised anything was wrong either.'

'Look, I'm sorry. I really am. But hang on, when you rang me last night from the hotel, didn't you say Lisa was there with you? Are you telling me that it happened since then? Today?'

Last night, Graham told him. They had been going out to eat somewhere else. 'She wouldn't eat here for some reason. We had a row, I stopped the car, we got out, carried on arguing. And she suddenly dived back in and drove off. She just left me there. I had to walk back. So she wasn't with me when you rang.' He shrugged his shoulders awkwardly. 'I didn't like to say. I thought she'd come back.'

Alan moved awkwardly. 'I'm sorry.

So where did she go?'

Jen was finding herself very aware of Alan and everything he did and said. There was a distance between the two men. Alan was holding himself apart from his brother's turmoil.

'No,' Graham said, brushing his eyes with his hand and ignoring the question. 'I'm fooling myself. This has been coming on a while and I've been unwilling to admit it. My own fault.' He looked up. 'But Alan, she's bound to want the house. I've nowhere to go. I wondered, since the tenants have moved out of Sellybrook, could I use it for a bolt-hole for a while? Until I can get myself straight?' He coughed, fist to mouth. 'I've been doing nothing but thinking, all last night. I couldn't sleep.'

Alan hesitated. 'No problem.' Perhaps his voice was a bit too enthusiastic. 'What are brothers for?'

Graham reached across to shake his hand. 'Thanks.'

'You don't think there's any chance of reconciliation? Did she give any reasons?' He added cautiously, 'You hadn't been having an affair, had you, Graham? Either of you?'

'Nothing like that. But she was always so full of anger. And she was on anti-depressants you know. Going back home, to Sellybrook, will do me so much good. I need to lick my wounds.'

'Understandable,' Alan muttered. He was frowning.

'I won't stay, now that I've seen you. And I've got a key for Sellybrook on my keyring. I've always carried it.' He smiled. 'Like a talisman.'

'What about transport, if Lisa took the car? And what about your things?' Alan was shaking himself into action as if coming out of a dream.

'You're right. I'll go home first and get my stuff. That will be best, won't it?'

'She can't object to that. But I wish you'd think again. Don't do anything you might regret later.' Alan was looking at his watch. 'Well, if I drop you at the station, I can easily be back in time for the reception. I think the hotel's in the same direction.' He glanced over to the bridal party, looking past Jen. 'Perhaps I should just have a quick word with David first.'

David? Yes, Pamela's new husband. And this could be her chance to be useful. Jen said, 'Is there a problem? If you would like me to pass on a message.'

'Thanks.' His smile was well worth the effort. 'That would be helpful. It would save time for me. I think it's best if we get off. I don't know how the traffic will be. Just tell David something's come up and I won't be long.'

He had accepted her intervention without question. Now Graham looked directly at her for the first time. He had soft, still eyes. The passive sort who would have put up with Lisa's quirks, Jen thought. 'Thank you. That's kind of you. And if you could apologise to the bride for my wife, Lisa and myself.'

'No,' Alan said, 'too complicated. I'll sort all that out when I get back.' His fingers were twitching round his car keys. 'Better go.'

Jen gave Graham a sympathetic smile. She wanted to tell him she knew, only too well, what Lisa was like and that perhaps things weren't as bad as he thought and above all, to wish him well, whatever happened. But Alan had a hand on his brother's shoulder, turning him from her and Jen could understand that he wanted to get Graham away. Weddings should be happy occasions. Graham and Lisa's problems had no place here. She smiled at Alan. 'Don't worry. I'll sort everything out and save you a place.'

No, she thought, watching the silver car driving off. Lisa must not spoil Pamela's day with her troubles. Whatever had she been thinking of? This must be what Lisa had wanted to talk about and trust her to go storming off without even trying to discuss it.

She turned away from the road and went to pass on her message — although of course by now Pamela had noticed Lisa's absence. Jen improvised and said she thought Lisa hadn't been feeling well, so her husband had taken her home. She managed to make it all sound very vague and Pamela seemed satisfied. They moved on to the hotel where the reception was to be held and Jen checked in and collected her key. 'Oh, and do you have a Mr Alan Littlewood staying here too?' He must have the same surname as Lisa. Yes, they had. She told them he had been slightly delayed.

By the time he returned, Jen had taken her bag upstairs, joined in with the photographs, wandered around the grounds and was wondering whether there had been a change of plan. Perhaps Alan had been persuaded to give Graham a lift all the way home — which was of course somewhere in Birmingham — and then on to Sellybrook, wherever that might be. It sounded as if that must have been the family home. If so, she would just have to write this encounter off. A missed opportunity. Just one of those things.

All the same, she would save him a seat. There didn't seem to be named place settings. She chose two at the large round table nearest the door and put her bag on the empty one while the tables filled with the other guests. And here he was, at last, in the doorway, looking round at the crowded room. She waved. Next to her, a lady in a pink hat murmured, 'What a good-looking man.' Jen smiled, feeling a whiff of pride — and also doubt. Was he too good-looking for her? Jim had been woefully ordinary and a sensible choice as her mother had said. But look where that had got her.

Alan had seen her. He smiled and his whole face lifted with pleasure and it was happening again. She felt that same heating of the flesh down her arms, a subtle changing inside herself somehow. And seeing him framed in the doorway against the green velvet curtains and the lights transmuting his fair hair to gold, Jen thought yes. This is the rest of my life.

Her neighbour's voice intruded into the moment, breathing sherry into her ear. 'Is he your husband?'

'Not yet.' Jen laughed. 'Sorry, no. Just a friend.' She turned to face him as he sat down, instantly forgetting everyone around them. 'Is everything all right?'

'Yes, thanks. My brother seems a bit shell-shocked, of course. But it may all blow over. They've had plenty of rows before; Graham may have been exaggerating a bit. Though it isn't like Lisa to miss something like this. She was set on coming — from what Graham told me. And apparently she gets depressed. Would that account for a change in behaviour?'

'I suppose it might. Although she never used to be.' Jen smiled at his surprise. 'Pamela and I were students with her. We've known her for years — though I haven't seen her for a while. And I know how annoying she can be.' Jen stopped; perhaps this wasn't quite fair. 'But she has her good points too. She can be warm and caring and she makes me laugh. I think she's only bossy because she does care and wants to be helpful.'

An odd expression crossed Alan's face. Wry acknowledgement maybe? He said, 'I know. Yes, I do know that. But if you're in touch with her, perhaps you could get to know her side of things? They have a good relationship usually. A pity if it should crumble over something that doesn't matter.'

'Doesn't everything?' Jen said. 'You get through disagreements about money and how to handle the in-laws and then everything flounders over toothpaste or burnt toast.'

He nodded. 'Is that the sad voice of experience?' He was looking into her eyes and surely he wasn't just pretending to be interested?

'Yes and no. We didn't have disagreements, Jim and I. We just carried on in a life where nothing much mattered or caused any excitement.' She smiled, confident in how well she was shielding her hurt. Everyone had been convinced, except her mother.

And Alan. 'I see.' His eyes were creased with sympathy and she knew that he did see. 'Being adult can be very painful, all the same.'

Somehow she found herself breaking all her resolutions and telling him all about Jim's betrayal. She talked until there was nothing else she could possibly say. She paused for breath at last, feeling cleansed and much much better. 'I'm sorry. That's all water under the bridge now and I've been busy sorting myself out. Everything's back on track. I moved back home with my mum, but I'm looking for a flat of my own.'

'Don't apologise. No point in bottling things up. I take it as a compliment that you feel able to share it with me. Do you want anything from the buffet?'

'Buffet? Goodness, yes, of course.' She laughed. 'There won't be anything left.'

'I'm sure we'll find something.' When

they had returned with plates of chicken legs and sausage rolls, he said, 'So you're going to be living alone again? Can be lonely when you're not used to it.'

'I'm looking forward to doing my own thing. Pleasing myself.'

'And I can't believe that an attractive woman like you will get the chance to be alone for long.' He grinned at her.

Jen choked on a piece of melon and turned aside to cough. 'Sorry, it's the way you raise one eyebrow like that.'

'I don't usually have that effect. I'll keep a firm control on both eyebrows from now on. So what do you do?'

'I'm a teacher. At present. I used to love it but now I feel totally drained.'

He picked up on that as she had intended and they had made their own island in the hot, chattering noise of the room, talking as if they couldn't stop, flitting from one topic to another and back again. As if they had known each other for years. Jen could never have imagined anyone more different from

18

Jim and his silences and the safe, solid world he stood for — which had all been a sham. Alan said, 'I've had one or two long-term relationships but I've never been able to make that final commitment. Perhaps it's been a psychological thing.'

'And why not, if you're happy with that? My mistake was in sliding into the long-term commitment because it seemed the thing to do.'

'I have been happy with that. Up to now.' He was no longer laughing. 'You have to learn to live in the present and make the most of it. And this present moment, right now, is looking good.'

She said quietly, 'It's looking good from where I am too.'

The dancing began and Alan gave no sign of leaving her side. Jen hugged Pamela as the happy couple circulated the tables. 'Stay happy,' she told her, willing her to do just that. And there seemed no reason to doubt that David and Pamela would be. The new husband was explaining to her how he worked with Alan, who had been his guide and mentor in his years at Fretwell's and had taught him everything. 'I had good material,' Alan said, 'and all I ask is you remember me when you get your directorship.' They all laughed. Only Pamela, pink with pride, believed the obvious exaggeration, but it had been a kindness to say it.

They danced all evening and hardly sat down. Jen had forgotten that she could be so energetic. They joined in with all the silly dances and laughed themselves giddy. Jen didn't even have time to top up on the wine and champagne. She'd forgotten how drunk you could feel purely on happiness.

Her stomach ached with laughing and they moved on to the slow dances and Alan slid his hand beneath her jacket, around her waist. She was aware of the heat of his fingers penetrating her thin top and burning her skin. 'I've never met anyone like you, Jen. Why didn't I meet you years ago?'

'But we've come together now,

haven't we? This is perfect. It seems greedy to ask for more.'

'Does it?' He was looking at her with that intense, questioning stare. As if he needed to know whether she felt the same way as he did.

She understood him. Her heart was beating faster. She whispered, 'I don't know. Maybe not.'

They had steered themselves into a corner where ornamental plastic trees shrouded a rear exit and his kiss was discreet and gentle. Returning it, Jen wouldn't have cared if they had been floodlit and centre stage. She was coming alive again.

They left before the dancing was over. His room was only across the corridor from hers. There were times when you knew things were right. Times when you had to seize an opportunity or lose something of immense value. She had never felt so happy.

She was still smiling as she woke the next morning, thinking at first that she was dreaming the warm body beside her. The new happiness flooded back as she remembered where she was and who she was with. No regrets, only a deep and intense joy. Jim was fading fast, like an old photograph left out in the sun. She sighed with contentment.

But there was something else too. Something that worried and gnawed at the back of her mind. Something she would have thought of before if she hadn't been so preoccupied with falling in love. She frowned and dismissed it, whatever it was.

Because yes, she had fallen in love. Now and forever. She was certain of it. If anyone had told her two days ago that this could happen, she would have laughed in disbelief. She could hardly believe that it was less than twenty-four hours since she had seen Alan for the first time. She felt as if she had known him for ever. She smiled at the memory of her first sight of him. Alan getting out of his car. The blocked bridge. And the worry surfaced and exploded. It had been growing all night, unobserved, and now could not be ignored.

A horrifying and unbelievable connection. Lisa had not turned up at the wedding. Someone had jumped off the bridge. Not Lisa? It couldn't be. Surely Lisa wouldn't have felt that badly about her marriage — and she would never have taken her own life. Not the Lisa Jen knew. But she had managed, successfully, to lose touch with Lisa lately. Both Graham and Alan had mentioned her depression. And now that Jen had fitted these facts together, she couldn't separate them.

No, this was ridiculous. Alan would tell her so. She only had to share her fears and he would dismiss them. She reached over to wake him.

Alan's phone rang. She jumped and her reaching hand became a nudge to alert him. Already he was rolling over to pick it up, smiling at her. 'Graham? What's wrong?' He frowned. 'That's odd. Where else would she go? But don't worry, I'm sure she'll turn up.'

Every muscle in Jen's body was frozen. She could hardly breathe.

Alan was still trying to sound reassuring but she knew him too well, already, to be convinced. 'Perhaps she's gone to stay with a friend, talk it all out, you know? Tell you what, get your stuff together and I'll come over and pick you up.' The words hung in the air between them as he switched off and put the phone down. 'Lisa hasn't gone home yet.'

'Oh, Alan.' Jen was unable to keep the horror from her face. Slowly she saw the realisation of it becoming reflected in his. She watched him working it out, coming to the same conclusion. She said, 'It's just a coincidence. It could have been anybody.'

But even then, they both knew it was not.

2

In her head Dorothy was already marking that Wednesday in her diary with a black circle. September 4th, 1985. When she was first married, she had filled in dozens of red circles, signifying joy in her own private code, but she hadn't done that for a long time now. She couldn't even remember where her red pen was.

But this had been a particularly dreadful day. The boys' pet rabbit had escaped onto the estate and got caught in a snare, and Malcolm had made them kill it themselves. She could still see the white, set faces. 'Can't you do it, Dad? Please?'

'When you own an animal, you take full responsibility for its welfare. And while you're messing about, wasting time, that dumb creature is suffering. And bleeding all over your school blazer. Your mother won't clean that up in a hurry. Get that large hammer out of the outhouse and get on with it.'

They had no choice. Dorothy went back into the hallway. When the boys came back, they couldn't speak. Dorothy took the blazer silently, her throat tight with tears. And at the tea table, the two boys sat quietly, not eating. Malcolm sent them upstairs. 'Namby-pambies, the pair of you. You're twelve and fifteen for heaven's sake. There are times when you have to be cruel to be kind.'

Now Malcolm was standing by the oak settle in the dining room, watching Dorothy as she cleared the table. It was unnerving and she had to concentrate, planning each action with care. He said, 'Dorothy, I'm leaving you.'

'Oh. Are you?' The pile of plates slid across the hand-embroidered table-cloth, a gift from Malcolm's mother. Two knives and a fork overbalanced onto the floor. Gravy splashed onto the pink silken daisies.

'Can't you be more careful?' Malcolm stooped to retrieve the cutlery with his fingertips, his mouth tight with distaste.

Dorothy swallowed. She must stay calm. Malcolm hated undue fuss. 'I'm not sure what you mean.'

'It's simple enough. This marriage hasn't turned out as I expected. Better all round if we call it a day.'

'But Malcolm, why?' She thought, I must stay calm. 'I know I can't help annoying you sometimes. But I've always done my best. You know that.'

He moved one hand quickly as if brushing at an insect. But she knew he was brushing her away. 'You'll be provided for. I've looked into it.'

She almost thanked him but that would be stupid, so stupid to be thanking him for the cold shock that was seeping through every limb like an injection at the dentist's. 'Have you met someone else?'

He stepped sideways and a bunch of dried teasels hanging from the low beam brushed his thick brown hair. 'Yes, as it happens. But that need not concern you. I would have gone anyway, eventually. Surely you knew that? What else did you expect? You only have to look at yourself, Dorothy.'

No doubt he hadn't intended being taken literally but she found herself obeying and seeing all too clearly where the grease spots had splashed across the cheap, print apron and up over her beige blouse. 'Is it someone I know?' she mumbled.

'Of course not. You don't know many people, do you? That's part of your problem — never going out, never making the effort.'

She turned to look out of the stone-edged window at the width of the drive and the trees. The shock had protected her for the first few moments but now the tears were forming. 'What are we going to tell the children?'

'They'll understand. They're sensible enough. They need toughening up a bit, that's all. Ideally, I would have waited until they had left school before making the move but now that I've met Elizabeth, the situation has changed. You must see that.'

It was no good. Misery was swelling within her like a stretched balloon and she could no longer contain it. She put her hands to her forehead, shaking her head from side to side. 'No, you can't do this to me, Malcolm. You can't, you can't.'

He sighed and she remembered afterwards, looking back on the scene in a mood of dull, morose calm, that he was smiling at last. As if her lack of control was justifying his opinion of her. He said, almost gently, 'I never meant to hurt you. I don't agree with the infliction of suffering. It will be for the best. For both of us.'

She would never believe that. And in the weeks that followed, when periods of intense grief alternated with bleak despair, only the children helped her to keep any semblance of balance.

Whatever would she have done without them?

I have my sons, Dorothy thought. They brought meaning into her life. Each day, seeing them off to school, she missed them. There was a rocky hillock to the side of their entrance, left by a long-ago glacier apparently. Each day, at half past four, she would climb it and watch for them as they walked along the lane from the bus stop in the village.

Today, she was even earlier than usual but the house had seemed so empty. She looked back at the long stone building, containing its own sunlight. She loved this view, looking back. I should be thankful, she thought. I have my boys and this house.

She turned back to the gateway as a car slowed to drive down the lane, the noise of the engine disturbing the stillness. A car down this lane was always an event. Beyond Sellybrook, there was only the Martonby Hall estate and since his wife had died,

Frank Parkestone had spent much of his time in London, or even with his properties in France. According to the gossip in the village shop, that was; Dorothy had never met him.

And this was nothing to do with the Parkestones, anyway. It was Malcolm's car. Her heart jolted. Perhaps this time he had changed his mind and was coming home. Her mouth was dry as she half-slid and half-stumbled downwards. She would have had her hair done if she'd known, would have changed out of these trousers at the very least. He was out of the car and frowning as she panted up to him. She said, 'Hello, Malcolm. This is a surprise. The boys will be pleased to see you.'

'It didn't seem appropriate to relay this information by letter or phone or third party. I felt I owed you that much. A solicitor can be the coward's way out.'

'I would have changed if I'd known. But I wore trousers for climbing the hill.'

'I've been looking into financial matters.' He glared down as his polished shoes scuffed the unraked gravel. 'Keeping two households on the go isn't easy. It's fortunate that there's a convenient solution.'

'What? What solution?'

'Selling the house, of course.' He spoke briskly, as if addressing an idiot. 'You must have realised that would be necessary? It's far too large for you. There are some nice new semis in the village, which would be ideal.'

She felt as if he had hit her. She could hardly believe that this was real. The shock was as great as when he had said he would leave. Greater, in fact. This house was her life, her home. 'No. I won't do it.' She didn't want to live anywhere else. She knew Malcolm's snobberies; he would never, never come back to her once she had moved to some modern semi-detached. And this house held her heart. 'It's my house, Malcolm.'

His head shot back. 'I think not.'

'It was my money. The money my grandmother left me.' More than enough for a hefty deposit and coming to her just as the right time. It had been meant, she had thought. Malcolm, the house, everything.

'But I paid off the mortgage.' There was triumph in his voice.

She said carefully, 'The boys love it here. Their home is their stability. You can't take it away. It's bad enough that they have been robbed of a father.'

He gave an exasperated sigh. 'Be sensible. Think about it. A big old rambling house like this is hardly suitable for someone of a nervous disposition. You're so isolated here, on your own.'

She laughed. That was ridiculous. 'But I'm not on my own.'

'Our sons won't be around for ever.'

In a moment of inspiration, she thought, why not? Yes, the house was too big for one person — but now suddenly she had a swift and wonderful vision of converting it into three separate homes, a small flat for herself tucked away somewhere, and the house filled with Alan and Graham and their wives and families. The golden stones echoing with children's laughter.

Malcolm was saying, 'They will grow up and move on. You have to think of the future. Besides, if you want stability for them, choose to live in Martonby village and they can still attend the same school. Or, even better, if we sold this there might even be a chance of the fees for Speeton Grammar. That would open all kinds of doors for them, and there's still time for Alan to benefit from the sixth form. That's worth considering, surely?' His smile was stiff and unconvincing.

'How can you say that? You're just making use of the boys to get your own way.'

He shook his head. 'This always happens when I try to have a logical discussion with you. This house is half mine, Dorothy, and the money will have to come from somewhere.'

She glared at him, sensing the tears again. She managed to say, 'Yes, it will. Somewhere else.'

'I had hoped to make everything easy for you. But this will have to go through the solicitor after all. If that's the way you want it.' He turned back to the car and was unlocking the door.

Dorothy swallowed, determined to sound sensible. 'The boys, Malcolm. They'll be here in a minute or two. Don't you want to wait?'

He shrugged. 'Remember what I've said. You have some hard thinking to do.' He manoeuvred the car with three controlled movements. As he reached the gateposts, the two figures were turning in. She saw Alan and Graham waving and thought he must surely stop. But he drove on.

*   *   *

'I don't see,' Erica said, checking her hat, 'why you have to be in such a rush. What's wrong with living together until you're sure? Everyone does it these days.'

A surreal conversation to be having with your mother, the rightful order of things turned on its head. Jen said, yet again, 'We are sure. I feel as if I've known Alan for years. And he does everything quickly, that's how he is. I love it. He makes me feel wild and reckless. Can I look in the mirror now, do you think?'

Erica moved to one side, still making unnecessary adjustments. 'He's one of those little-boy men, that's his trouble. He doesn't think.'

Jen grinned. Her mother couldn't help this continual gloom, she knew that. It was how she was. It didn't matter. Today, nothing mattered. She had never been so happy. 'Perhaps you should just be pleased that we've invited you. We could just have slipped away and told you afterwards. That was what Alan wanted to do.' Because he hadn't wanted to invite Graham. It would have been too much for him, after all the sadness of Lisa's funeral and inquest, the official recognition that her death had been suicide. Alan hadn't wanted to parade his own happiness in front of his grieving brother. Jen could understand that.

And at first after Lisa's death, Alan too had been in a very dark and silent place. With Jen's love and support he had gradually recovered and become again the person she had first met. She intended to make sure he never went back there.

Her mother was saying, 'I suppose it makes sense to have a quiet wedding, second time around. Look at the expense of the first one, and for what?'

Jen gave her a quick hug. 'Not another word. As a topic, that's banned, OK? Just for today, if you can manage it.' Her phone bleeped.

'I should turn that off now if I were you,' Erica said helpfully.

'It may be Alan.' It wasn't. She opened up the text message. Her hand tightened around the phone until her fingers ached. 'Wish I could be with U today. Wishing U every happiness. Lisa x.'

Far away, her mother's voice was saying, 'What's the matter? I knew it. Has he changed his mind?'

Somehow, her mouth said, 'No. It's nothing. Not Alan at all. A mistake.'

'One of those scams where somebody tries to sell you something. Turn it off.'

'Yes.' It must have been a mistake. Surely. An unfortunate, dreadful coincidence, a wrong number from someone with the wrong name. She switched the phone on again. She should check where the message had come from. Her fingers seemed to have grown into puffballs. Lisa's phone. That had been Lisa's number. She switched it off, wishing she hadn't thought about checking it. That had only made things worse. Stay calm.

'Never happier than when you're glued to a tiny screen,' Erica was saying. 'I knew you wouldn't turn it off. And the taxi's here.'

She went through the motions of collecting her posy, locking the door, getting into the taxi automatically. Only as they set off did she manage to recover rational thought. Somebody had got hold of Lisa's phone, that was all. She didn't even know what had happened to it. At the inquest, they had heard how the police had found the car down near the stream, out of sight on a track in the woodlands. Lisa's handbag had been in some bushes, as if thrown there. Listening, Jen had pictured the unhappy Lisa hiding the car and climbing back up the steep track to the stone arch of the bridge above. Had her phone been in the bag? It had never been mentioned, not specifically. If Lisa had thrown the bag into the bushes, the phone could have fallen out. There were any number of explanations of how it could have fallen into the wrong hands.

Yes, that would be it. And after the wedding was over, because she refused to waste any more time and emotion on the sick character who had done this, she would share it with Alan and he would banish her fears at once. That was something he was incredibly, wonderfully good at. Always seeing the obvious explanation she might have missed.

But after the wedding was over, it no longer seemed that important. She pushed the nasty little incident away and forgot all about it. Until the next message came.

3

I have to stop him, Dorothy thought. Once again she was watching from her vantage point by the gate as the boys walked along the lane to the bus stop. I have to keep my house. Our house.

The postman's van slowed to avoid the two walking figures and passed her own gateway before driving on towards Martonby Hall. She could see flashes of red as the van began the long trek up the tree-lined drive. There was no need for Dorothy to hurry back; it would be a good five minutes before the postman arrived back at her door.

She paused, frowning. For a moment, she had felt on the brink of a new idea. No, it had gone.

The sense of missing an opportunity niggled at her all morning. Do something else, she told herself, and it would come back to her — but an unnecessary

41

round with the Hoover didn't help. So she went back to her hillock where the idea had first hovered and sat on her favourite rock, hugging her knees as the sun warmed her back. It was comfortable here. She could stay here all day if she felt like it, until the boys came back again. At least until she felt hungry. She could have brought sandwiches. She smiled at herself. Her panic since Malcolm's visit was subsiding. Sitting here, his threat seemed unreal.

She could be getting on with the garden, she supposed. Before Malcolm's bombshell, she had been making so many plans. Malcolm had left a legacy of control. She would cut down most of the privet that lined the drive and plant golden banks of potentilla and hypericum. And throw out Malcolm's neat rows of gladioli spears and the regimented dahlias — and that neat little square of lawn by the house could be made into a herb garden with wandering paths. Graham would help her with that; he seemed interested in plants and their properties and she wondered, fondly, whether he might eventually have a career in pharmacy — if he didn't become an artist.

The Martonby Hall Mercedes came along the lane, gliding past her own woodland, windows glinting as it swept onwards below her. Her eyes followed the sleek, dark shape, just as she had watched the post van. A nuisance for the Parkestone family, she thought, always having to loop around the Sellybrook land in that way. Not at all direct or convenient. Probably something to do with ancient boundaries and pathways.

Yes. She turned her head slowly, scanning the landscape where the Martonby estate backed onto her small patch of marshy woodland. That was it. That was the idea which had been eluding her. She put both hands to her face, amazed at the simplicity of it.

She must act on this at once. She knew Frank Parkestone was in, didn't she? She had just seen his car. But he might be busy. Perhaps she should make an appointment. No, she must go now, while she could be carried along by the exhilaration of the idea, lending her courage.

Dorothy slithered down the hillock. Should she change? She had that svelte black suit that Malcolm had insisted on for smart lunches in town but she had never liked it; she always felt as if she was dressing up as someone else.

No, she would be sensible and workmanlike, in her plain skirt and warm stockings and beige wool jacket. Walk or drive? The footpath was quicker but might be muddy. It was quite a long way round by the drive, that was the whole point.

She took the car. The Martonby drive was narrow and unfamiliar. She drove slowly and braked sharply as a young man with a gun over his shoulder and a spaniel at his heels came out of the dense leaves of the rhododendrons to cross the drive in front of her. He was glowering straight ahead, not looking at her.

Far too young to be Mr Parkestone. The son, perhaps? She knew very little about the Parkestones beyond what she had overheard in the shop and had tried not to listen to that because Malcolm had disapproved of gossiping chit-chat.

The Mercedes was still by the front door. Oh, dear, did that mean that Mr Parkestone was intending to go out again? She didn't want to be in the way. She parked carefully to one side of the drive, thought again and reversed a little.

A figure appeared beside her, bending down to the car window. And of course it was the young man from the drive. She struggled with the handle. 'Will I be all right here? Not in the way?'

The peak of his tweed cap shadowed the angular face. 'Hardly.' He was very 'hunting-and-shooting', as Malcolm would have said.

Her face was burning. 'Is your — is Mr Parkestone in?'

45

'As far as I know. You'll have to knock and ask.'

Dorothy wished he would go away. He was putting her off, watching her like that. She fiddled in her handbag, found a tissue and dabbed at her nose but he didn't move. This was ridiculous; he couldn't be much more than eighteen or nineteen from what she had heard. She was old enough to be his mother. Wasn't she? Much older than he was anyway — but he had the arrogant confidence that accompanied wealth. Whatever would his father be like?

He wasn't going to go. She got out of the car and had a brief impression of pillars, black paintwork and a Georgian frontage. How many servants would there be inside and all sneering at her? Oh, she should have phoned first. And now she couldn't see the bell. Oh, there it was. How silly of her. She pressed it, as firmly as she could.

⋆ ⋆ ⋆

The phone rang and Jen dropped Alan's new nutmeg-grating gadget, an impulse buy from a new internet site. At last. She had been trying to get hold of him ever since she got back from work, having had his text at lunchtime. Everything had been signed on the latest development property, and things were going well. As promised that morning, she had cooked a special meal in celebration and opened a bottle of red wine. Now he was ringing to tell her what time he would be arriving.

She snatched at the phone without bothering to look at the screen, and avoiding the cat that was mewing round her ankles. 'Ssh, Dinah. Hello Alan.'

'Sorry.' The woman's voice sounded amused. 'I'd like to speak to Alan Littlewood myself, please.'

'I'm afraid he isn't here. Have you tried his mobile?' Perhaps it was to do with the sale. She glanced at the casserole, out of the oven for tasting.

'Not switched on. I left a voicemail but he hasn't got back to me.'

'I'm sorry about that,' Jen said in her professional voice but smiling ruefully. A common failing with Alan. She sometimes wondered how anyone got to speak to him at all. 'Can I take a message?'

'Yes. I think you'd better. Tell him I'm calling about my cousin, Lisa Littlewood. She died last year.'

Jen stared as the phone, as if that would help somehow. 'Cousin?' She couldn't remember Lisa mentioning a cousin — but then, Jen also had cousins who had never come into the conversations either. Why would they? 'Yes. I'm so sorry. A dreadful shock. Shall I take your name?'

'I wanted to tell Alan that I'm not happy about Lisa's death. Not happy at all.'

'Of course not. No. Were you at the funeral?'

'Unfortunately not. Nor the inquest. I was working in Spain at the time.'

'I'm sorry about that.' Jen tried to sound sympathetic. 'That must have been awful. I'll certainly tell him you rang. If you could just give me your name.'

'I think he'll know who I am.'

Jen frowned. 'Will he?' Why not tell her instead of playing these guessing games? She had a sudden thought. 'I don't suppose you've been sending me text messages, have you?'

The surprise sounded genuine. 'Text messages? How could I? I don't know your mobile number. Anyway, I'll be waiting to hear from Alan. As soon as possible. Goodbye.'

'Goodbye,' Jen said, to the dialling tone. Yes, she was sure she was right. This mystery cousin obviously had some bee in her bonnet and had got hold of Lisa's phone somehow. It was a very plausible explanation. Though why she should have been targeting Jen for her sick jokes was beyond belief. Perhaps she had expected Jen to tell Alan and been very disappointed when nothing had happened? Yes, that would be it. Well, she would decide when to pass on the enigmatic message — if she bothered at all. She wasn't going to have this woman interfering with her casserole.

And once Alan arrived, all such little annoyances went out of her head. He was telling her how the purchase had gone through and their plans for the property. 'Perhaps another one, two max, and we can go in for developing full time, both of us. That's what you want, isn't it?'

'Certainly is.' She was spooning the casserole onto the plates, adding a sprig of fresh mint. 'I've had enough of being inspected by Ofsted every five minutes and doing all that paperwork.'

Alan poured the wine. 'This smells amazing. So, here we go. Let's drink to the future and new opportunities.'

Jen raised her glass as the phone rang again. 'Oh, no. I meant to put the answer phone on. A mystery woman's been trying to get hold of you. Said she was Lisa's cousin but wouldn't give her name. I can disconnect us if you like.'

'It's OK,' Alan said easily. 'I'll handle it. Alan Littlewood here.'

Jen tried a mouthful of the lamb, wondering if the sauce really went with the wine. Never mind; after a few mouthfuls, neither of them would notice. Watching Alan's face and the way his forehead became tight, she forgot to chew.

He was saying, 'Yes, of course I remember.' Casual and easy, just as if he hadn't had that initial reaction. He grinned at Jen, raising his eyebrows and shaking his head. 'That's right. Yes, I see. It is.' He was twisting his face into grotesque expressions now. Jen giggled. 'I'll get back to you.' He put the phone down on the table. 'Where were we?'

Had he been talking to someone else? Jen said, 'Was it that woman? Didn't she ask you about Lisa? She told me she wasn't happy about Lisa's death.' No, the sauce was wrong. Too peppery. She didn't remember adding pepper.

He was talking as he ate. 'Did she? Oh, yes. Nothing to worry about. She's

Lisa's cousin. She was working in Spain selling holiday villas or something at the time and didn't get to the inquest or the funeral.'

'I can see how that would upset her. But why ring you? And you didn't seem to be telling her much.' Jen stopped. Alan was beginning to look defensive. 'I didn't mean that as a criticism. I'm just hoping that she isn't going to be pestering you about this.'

'Forget about her. It's nothing.' He raised his glass once more. 'So, to us and to our new future. Our very new future. And — there's been a bit of a change of plan.'

'Has there?' This was Alan all over. She smiled in anticipation.

'Oh, yes. You know how the purchase of Number 86 has just gone through? I didn't tell you when I came in, was keeping it for a bit of a surprise. But it's no good, I can't keep it in any longer.'

'And?' she laughed. 'Forget the dramatic effect. Just tell me.'

'Well, I've been offered ten thousand more, without lifting a hammer or wielding a paintbrush. Money for doing nothing. So I've accepted it.'

Jen blinked. 'That is a surprise. You clever thing.'

'And — I tell you, it's all been happening today — I've had a great tip-off about some good properties that are coming up. Near Leeds.' He leaned forwards, taking her hand. 'How do you fancy moving north? It's the way forward. I'm convinced of it.'

It was mad, unpredictable. Joy burst in Jen's mind like a firework fountain. 'Sounds brilliant.' Impossible not to be swept away by Alan's enthusiasm. Exciting. She was more than happy to go with it; they'd talked about making changes. Just not quite so soon.

'You don't mind going north?'

'Of course not. Whither thou goest I will go, where thou lodgest I will lodge.' What was that from? The Bible? 'It's from the book of Ruth, isn't it? So not totally appropriate, I suppose, as it's about a mother-in-law and daughter-in-law, isn't it?'

Alan seemed strangely still. 'I don't know much about the book of Ruth.'

Somehow Jen sensed she had said the wrong thing. He hardly ever mentioned either of his parents. Stupid of her. She said cheerfully, 'But the sentiments are completely appropriate. I think I heard the story at infant school. If you're going to Yorkshire, so am I. It will be fun. A new challenge. And I'm sure Dinah will love it.'

The awkward moment passed and was forgotten. But later, Jen realised her slip had distracted her from something else. An inconvenient niggle was worming its way into her head. Just as if her mother was at her side, giving an unwelcome opinion. Had Alan really intended to surprise her? Everything he had said when he first came in had given not the slightest hint of it. The conversation had been so detailed, following on from everything they had agreed earlier.

It was almost as if that phone call had been the turning point. A new start. Yes. So why did she have an uneasy feeling that they would be running away from something?

4

The door opened at once, almost before Dorothy had heard the bell ringing inside. The butler must be horribly efficient, she thought, trying to smile at the tall, grey-haired man with stooping shoulders. A typical retainer.

'It's the lady from next door, isn't it? I recognise the car.' He stepped back. 'Do come in. I'm Frank Parkestone.' He was smiling and his eyes seemed kind. Dorothy knew he had understood her mistake, didn't mind and was sparing her further embarrassment. How could you tell so much from one smile? But she was sure she was right. Her legs felt weak with the relief. She had done it. She was actually inside.

Chessboard floor, large, light windows. Otherwise, she hardly noticed where they were going as he led her across the square hall and into a room which was furnished in faded greens and creams. He proffered a chair, rearranging a cushion and the fabric beneath was darker, almost bottle-green. 'I'm sorry, it's chilly in here. I was just going to light the fire. At least it's set. All ready you see.'

'Oh, please — not for me. I mean, it doesn't matter.'

'It won't take a minute.' He knelt to put a flame to the crumpled paper with a silver cigarette lighter and talked on in a gentle, calming voice. He was saying something about landscaping and the Parkestone family history. Safe, impersonal topics to put her at her ease.

She said, 'I hope you don't mind my coming in person. This is a business call rather than a social one.'

'Of course I don't mind. And it could easily be both if you like.'

Dorothy knew she was raising her eyebrows. Was he making a joke? She was never sure, with strangers, whether they were joking or not. 'It occurred to me that you might consider purchasing our far stretch of woodland. You know, the piece that joins the lane near the village and connects with your land behind our house? It would be so much easier for you if you had another entrance and could bypass the lane. Don't you think?'

He laughed. 'If you only knew how my grandfather had argued over that very piece of land — and the house too. A long-standing issue between the two families for many years; your house, Sellybrook, had been left in the female line. A situation that often occurs when cousins inherit. It can lead to all kinds of problems.'

'Oh, so this isn't a new idea at all,' Dorothy said awkwardly. 'I expect you could have bought the land when Sellybrook first came on the market, when we bought it. If you'd wanted to.' Her throat was tight with disappointment. 'I hadn't thought of that.'

'No, no — because Mrs Laurence, your predecessor, was the last of the die-hard family members and wouldn't sell to us under any circumstances. If she couldn't have a true-born Laurence, she would rather sell out of the family altogether.'

'The old lady? But she seemed so kindly and hospitable when we went to view.'

'I'm sure she was. I never met her myself, which just shows how fierce these old family feuds can be. In fact I believe there's a covenant in place against any member of my family purchasing the house in the future.'

'Oh, I wouldn't be selling the house. No, definitely not. That's the whole point. I have to keep the house. It's just the land. That piece of land. But if it's not possible . . . ' And it had seemed such a heaven-sent plan. She tried not to blink. If she did, the tears would escape.

'I didn't say that and covenants can sometimes be circumvented, if you know where to go. And I doubt whether the land would be affected. Let's hope the wily old Mrs Laurence didn't manage to tie up every loose end. Yes, I may very well be interested, my dear. How much are you asking?'

She couldn't cope with his kindness. She fought against the tears and lost, furious with herself. She found a tissue and scrubbed at her face. 'I'm so sorry.'

'That's all right. I know you've had a tough time.'

Dorothy nodded, warily. 'Yes.'

'I don't mean to pry but I do know your husband has left you and your sons on your own.'

She smiled. He was so sympathetic that taking offence would be impossible. 'I suppose it's common knowledge by now. I suppose you go into the village shop too? That's where all the local news is distributed.'

'I'm afraid so. I've been known to pop in from time to time. And we have Mrs Slater who 'does'. If you want a private life, never live in a village. I don't mind it myself. People need people.'

'Yes, you're quite right. Thank you.'

She put the tissue away and fastened her bag. 'I'm all right now.'

'When I first heard about your situation, I wanted to do something but didn't like to interfere. I've been wondering what to do for the best, like a silly old fool.' He rested his hands on the soft arms of the chair. Every unhurried movement he performed suggested ease and calm. Dorothy just wanted to sit there for ever, drinking him in. He said, 'If you should ever want to talk about it, I'm always here you know.'

She didn't reply straight away, surprised that someone of Frank's status should trouble to make such an offer — and to her, of all people. He leaned forwards, his eyes anxious. 'No, I'm intruding. I'm sorry.'

'Oh, no, no.' She gabbled the words, horrified that she might seem to be rejecting his thoughtfulness. 'I do need someone to talk to, you can't know how much. I can talk to the boys about most things, they're both so mature for their ages, but I can't talk about their father, can I? That wouldn't be fair.'

'Quite right.'

'And the boys need the continuity of their school if nothing else. They're doing so well at Lower Shaw. I know it's a comprehensive, but very well regarded. Malcolm is talking about Speeton, as an incentive I suppose because he wants me to sell the house. But it would only unsettle them, surely?'

'My son Simon was a weekly boarder at Speeton, but I'm not convinced that it did him a great deal of good. Boarding seemed the best option when my wife died. Academically it's excellent but he's turned out sadly self-important, which may or may not be due to his school environment.' He sighed. 'I only wanted to do my best for him.'

'Oh, I'm sure you did. It may just be a phase he's going through.'

'Yes, indeed. And Oxford may improve him although it's early days yet and he's hardly ever there, it seems to me. Mooches about here far too much. I thought students spent their time going to wild parties and getting drunk.' He laughed. 'I shouldn't be advocating such activities, should I?'

'And if he went to parties like that, you'd be wishing he wasn't.' Dorothy wondered whether he was kindly exaggerating his own problem in order to take her mind of hers.

'I know. I'm hard to please, aren't I? But talking about it to a sympathetic audience is doing me good. Thank you, Dorothy. And now tell me again, in detail, about Malcolm and the house, because we must see what can be done.'

She obeyed and as she spoke seemed to become caught up in her whole life story. She talked quickly, not wanting to waste his time, but needing to tell him everything. He sat in silence, nodding encouragement. At last she sat back, with a deep liberating sigh. 'Thank you.'

'I haven't done anything yet.'

'For listening.'

'Oh, I'm good at listening. But perhaps I can help in other ways too. You haven't mentioned a solicitor in all of this. You do have one?'

'Yes. But I'm afraid I haven't been to see him yet. He's the one Malcolm and I had together. Malcolm used to handle everything.'

He shook his head. 'I'll put you onto someone else, if you'll allow me to, as that would be far better for you. You need someone who will act in your best interests. And I have no personal experience of divorce, but I suspect that your husband is talking nonsense about your having to sell. We can look into that.'

'I've been so used to trusting Malcolm and not thinking for myself.'

'But apart from all that, I'm more than willing to take the land if you're sure that's what you want. No need to make any kind of decision about that straightaway. Let's get your situation sorted out to begin with. So would you like me to get in touch with my lawyer? Shall I phone him now?'

Dorothy could hardly contain her happiness. 'Yes, please.'

★　★　★

The small rooms were filled with sound, something haunting from back in the eighties that Jen didn't immediately recognise — but she knew at once that Alan wasn't there. The house felt empty. She was already on edge; only a short car journey from the station after collecting her mother and she'd looked forward to this first visit but already Erica's presence was wearing thin.

'Smaller than I expected,' Erica said. 'I suppose it's all you can manage now that you've lost your security. Pleasant enough — but is it really suitable for raising a family?'

Jen ignored her. 'Alan? Hello?' She pressed a switch and the room was silent.

'He's not here.' Erica flicked her

handbag onto the nearest chair and began to unfasten her mack. 'It's just like the *Mary Celeste*. Don't worry, he'll be dashing off somewhere and forgotten to tell you about it. Just like Alan. Perhaps he's left a note.' She was off into the kitchen. 'No, nothing in here. No clues, except that he's put his dinner onto a plate and left it.'

'He was going to eat early,' Jen said absently. If he had left a note, she thought, it would have been on the coffee table. Sometimes he thought to do that. Or he would have texted her. And there was the meeting at half past. Surely he would be back for that? It had been his idea. Or something suggested by his contact at the estate agency, who had found them this house. Too good an opportunity to miss from what Alan had told her. There was a cold uneasy feeling crawling down her back. She said cheerfully, 'You're right, something's cropped up. I've got your food all ready here to pop in the microwave. But I'll have to go to a meeting I'm afraid. Still, I won't be long and Alan will be back soon I'm sure.'

'When are you going to eat?'

'When I get back.' Somehow, Jen wasn't hungry.

'What kind of meeting is it?'

'It's the AGM of the Local History Society. Doesn't sound too promising I know — but the chairman used to be in the planning department apparently. And there are other members with all kinds of information on suitable properties. It's well worth a try.' She waited for the inevitable criticism of this flimsy idea.

Erica said, 'Do you know, I think I'll come too. I like a good meeting. And I had a sandwich on the train because I wasn't sure whether you would have anything ready or when I would get it. So I'm fine.'

Perhaps it was for the best. Jen wouldn't have to worry about what Erica would be saying to Alan, left on her own with him. Although Alan thankfully seemed to find her amusing rather than annoying. 'OK. I'll get your bag out of the car.'

She ushered her mother upstairs, showed her the spare room, cut short the remarks about its smallness and the grudging acceptance of the view. What was the name of that man from the planning department she was supposed to talk to? Alan had written it down somewhere, hadn't he? She recalled him waving a piece of paper, emphasising his point of how useful this meeting would be. Perhaps he'd pushed it into a pocket and it was with him, wherever he was. But there was time for a quick look while Erica was in the bathroom. In the desk maybe. And there were contact cards in there somewhere; those would have been useful.

The desk was not at all as she had left it. Alan must have had one of his lightning reorganisation sessions. Fine — if he had been there to explain the new arrangement. And she didn't have time to go through it systematically. She pulled several drawers open and envelopes and bills and receipts showered down onto the floor, as if released by a spring. Never mind, she would have to try and restore the new filing system later. She scooped up a handful and tried to stuff them back, hampered by one of the drawers not opening properly. Something was stuck. She didn't have time for this. She tugged strongly and a photograph flew out and landed face down.

Jen turned it over and picked it up, frowning. It was Lisa. Why on earth would Alan have a picture of Lisa in the desk?

Erica was coming down the stairs. 'Aren't you ready yet? I thought we were in a hurry.'

The photograph stuck to Jen's fingers and she pushed it into her shirt pocket. She would ask him later, maybe. Put it back in this mess and she would never find it again. 'Yes, I'm fine. We can walk. It's not far. It's only in the community centre.'

She welcomed the cooling breeze that whipped up over the ridge as they walked. The village of Birkedge straggled above the industrial sprawl in the valley below, but behind them, where the land levelled out, were fields with cows and sheep. Alan had been right. This hadn't been what she had expected when Alan had suggested the north. She loved it here already.

The road was quiet. Somehow she had been expecting the whole village to be flocking to this meeting. She was beginning to wonder whether they had been told the wrong date and time but no, the double doors of the community centre were open in welcome. Inside, a handful of people were setting out cups and saucers on a table or arranging rows of chairs. Was this it? If she had thought they would be lost in a crowd, she had been mistaken. And how best to quietly introduce the topic of property developing and town planning?

No need to worry. Again, she had

never considered how the committee members' eyes would light up at the sight of them. Volunteers were obviously few and far between. That would explain the sparse attendance no doubt. She was asked in the first five minutes by a friendly woman who introduced herself as Helen Matthews, whether she might consider joining the committee. Jen explained that as a newcomer, perhaps they had better find their feet first, attend a few of the talks — there would be talks, she supposed? 'And we are pretty tied up with our property-developing business at the moment,' she said, 'on the lookout all the time for new opportunities. If you hear of anything for sale . . . ' Was she being too obvious? 'And you never know. About the committee.'

She should talk to Maria, she was told. Maria knew all about property — that was her job. But she hadn't arrived yet. And what about the old blacksmith's cottages? The heirs were desperate to sell — needing a fair bit of work but nothing too major. One or two others, joining in, suggested possibilities in the neighbouring villages. Somebody recommended a local builder.

This was better than Jen had hoped for. Perhaps, if there was a post on the committee that wasn't too onerous, she just might volunteer, to show willing. Just because they were all being so helpful.

When the chair called the meeting to order, pointedly closing the doors, she even remembered that he was the one who was the planning contact. Harold Matthews, that was it. He must be Helen's husband. In spite of the small attendance, the meeting seemed to proceed fluently without any awkward silences where people looked at the floor. Everyone in office seemed to be willing to continue. That was a relief. Jen was beginning to relax, knowing Alan would be pleased with what she had achieved. And of course he would be there waiting when they got back.

She didn't know what she had been worrying about. She only needed to have a quick word with Harold afterwards over the cups of tea and everything would be sorted.

The double doors opened with a flourish. A slim dark-haired woman in black with a green and blue scarf entered. A ripple of pleasure ran through the room. 'Hello Maria,' Harold said jovially. 'We were beginning to think we would have to minute you as an apology.'

'I'm so sorry, everyone.' A flash of warmth contrasting with the formal tone from the chair. And knowing, Jen thought, as the smiles broke out that everyone would forgive her. 'I ran over someone's cat, you see — couldn't be helped — owner distraught — had to give them a lift to the vet's — couldn't find the vet since I've never needed one — you know the kind of thing.'

Helen's eyes were wide with sympathy. 'That's terrible. What a shock for you. Is the cat all right?'

'Absolutely fine. Must have just been stunned, that's all.' She was taking a notebook and pen from her bag. 'I won't hold you up. Where had you got to?'

There was something familiar about her, Jen thought but she was certain they'd never met. She would have remembered. Black hair streaked with bright auburn, the colourful scarf relieving the graceful black of the tight sweater and jeans.

Harold smiled. 'Item Six. And of particular interest to you, Maria — the September outing.'

Maria sat straight in her chair, turning to face Harold directly. 'Actually, I've been thinking about that.'

'Good. I'm sure we're all looking forward to hearing what you have planned this year. Especially since it's the fifth year since we were founded.'

'That's just it. It needs to be something special and I'm right out of ideas. I think it needs someone else.'

Harold frowned, tapping his fountain

pen on the table. 'You're not thinking of relinquishing the position of events secretary, are you? Because if so you should have notified the chair in writing before the meeting commenced.'

'No, of course not. I wouldn't do that. I was thinking more of new blood, new ideas.' She turned to look at Jen and Erica, all too obvious on the second row. 'Perhaps a job share?'

'I've already asked them,' Helen said. 'They're not ready yet.'

Erica nudged Jen with her elbow. Without even looking at her, Jen knew she would be shaking her head. But why not? One day out shouldn't be too difficult or time-consuming. And if she did something for the village, the villagers would be more willing to help her in return. She said, 'I don't see why not. Just as a one-off.'

As she had hoped, the offer went down well. Harold and Maria both thanked her; Harold asked if one of them would let him know as soon as the venue had been decided, had no response for any other business and closed the meeting. As they all moved over to the refreshments, Maria appeared at her elbow. 'Thanks. That will be really helpful.'

'That's OK.' Jen grinned, knowing that she would be hearing the exact opposite from her mother all the way home.

'And I didn't realise before. We've spoken on the phone. You're Alan Littlewood's wife.'

Jen stared at her, her stomach contracting. She thought, she's found us. No wonder the woman had seemed familiar. Jen had recognised her voice. And Jen had thought she was being so clever, buying a new mobile phone to get rid of the text messages, together with moving all the way up here. She tried to speak normally. 'I remember. Lisa's cousin. You didn't tell me your name.'

'I know. I'm sorry. The whole thing was traumatic for me.'

'For all of us. I'm sorry you couldn't make the funeral. That was the problem, wasn't it? Because you were working abroad; was that what you said?'

'I didn't come to the funeral because no one thought to tell me about it. Or not in time. I could have got back easily, given sufficient notice.'

'I'm afraid I don't know anything about that. Alan and I didn't have anything to do with notifying people. You would have to speak to Graham about it. Lisa's husband.'

Maria patted her arm. 'I know. It's hardly Alan's fault if Graham won't communicate with me. I've allowed myself to get so uptight over the way Lisa died. And it's such a relief, meeting someone who'll be on my side and understand my point of view.'

Jen almost asked her who did she mean? Who was going to be on her side? Before realising Maria meant her. She shook her head, half wanting to be helpful but not certain what was being asked. 'About what?'

'You were there too, weren't you? At

77

that wedding when Lisa died? When you told me you had been a friend of Lisa's, I couldn't believe my luck.'

'Yes, I was. I'd known Lisa for years. And yes I'll talk to you.' What else could she say? What harm could it do? 'I doubt whether I'll be able to say anything helpful. It's all been fully reported.'

'Thanks. This is one of the reasons why getting together with you on the outing project is going to be so brilliant.' Maria lowered her voice. 'We can meet up as often as we like, without causing any suspicion.'

'Oh, now — just a minute.' Jan stared at her. 'Who's going to be suspicious? And of what?'

'No,' Maria said quickly, 'I didn't mean that exactly. Wrong choice of word. I just meant — ' She paused and laughed. 'Well, I don't quite know what I meant. It's the police terminology, isn't it? In suspicious circumstances. And I'd really appreciate it if I could talk to you on your own.'

'I expect so.' The photograph of Lisa was still burning against Jen's heart. She felt an irrational urge to cover her pocket with her hand, to prevent Maria suspecting it was there. She wished she hadn't brought it with her. But there was bound to be a rational explanation for that. She and Alan would be laughing about it tonight. When he turned up.

Maria was saying, 'It isn't only Graham. Alan keeps blocking me out too. More often than not, I can't get hold of him.'

'He doesn't like talking about it. Surely you can understand that?' Even if he had chosen to speak to her, Alan was expert at avoiding unwelcome topics, sliding off into alternative subjects. 'That's his choice.'

'Of course. I don't want to be pushy. There will be no need for us to worry Alan about it, I'm sure. So — we'll get together ASAP and I'll show you my list of all the destinations we've covered already. And we can work out somewhere new to go. I'm at my wits' end, I can tell you. I wasn't exaggerating.' Maria glanced at her watch. 'Oops, must dash. People to see.'

'What do you make of that?' Erica said.

'She seems pleasant enough,' Jen said lightly, gulping at her coffee and putting it down on the table. 'And now I have someone to see. I won't be long.' Although she had already decided that speaking to Harold must consist of no more than a handshake and a 'lovely to meet you all'. He was the last kind of person to be opening the back doors to planning. Any suggestion of it would cause offence. You'd think Alan's informant would have known that.

They could set off at last, with Erica talking to herself about Maria and the folly of Jen's offer. Jen said suddenly, 'Dinah! Did you see her when we got back home? Was she upstairs? She likes the spare bed.'

'The cat? No, no sign of her. But I was saying — oh! You think that woman might have run over your cat? But why should she? There are dozens of cats around; it could have been anyone's.'

Jen was remembering: owner distraught — had to run them to the vet's. That's what Maria had said. It would explain Alan's absence. She began to walk faster. And whatever would Alan have thought when he realised it was Maria? When he had been trying to avoid her, assuming he had?

'Anyway, she said the cat was fine, didn't she? There's no need to worry. Can't we slow down?'

Jen was almost jogging as she reached their gate with her mother panting behind her and her heart was thudding as if it had jumped out of her chest and taken on a life of its own, like a cartoon heart. Thump, thump, thump. She had her keys in her hand, praying that she wouldn't need them and this time her hand slid on the handle easily and the door was open. 'Alan, you're back!

Whatever happened?'

He was standing in the hall as if he'd heard them on the path, brushing a hand through the thick light hair and frowning and smiling alternately. 'I would have come on — but I thought I'd better stay here with Dinah.'

'Yes. Is she all right? Where is she?'

Dinah was curled smugly in her basket. Jen knelt down beside her, feeling the furry limbs gently as Dinah purred. 'She seems OK, doesn't she? How did it happen? Why didn't you leave me a note? Or text me?'

Alan put his arm round her shoulders. 'I'm sorry, I didn't think. There wasn't time. I thought it was a lot worse. I heard a car hooting and brakes squealing and then there was this woman at the door with the cat in her arms. There seemed to be blood and when she offered to take us to the vet, I just went with it.' He said softly, 'I couldn't bear to think of you coming home and finding Dinah had been hurt.'

Jen hugged him. 'I know. It must have been a shock.'

'And did you realise who the woman was?' Erica chipped in.

'Sorry? She didn't tell me her name. Hello, Erica. Did you have a good journey?'

Jen was feeling as if she had been given a collection of different bits of information that wouldn't fit together. And Alan had obviously been affected by the surprise of the incident; who wouldn't be? He had been thinking mainly of Jen. 'Don't worry about it, Alan. It must have been awful. We're not going to interrogate you.' She flashed her mother a warning look and put her arms round him. Because this wasn't wholly about the cat, was it?

But perhaps it would be OK. Perhaps in the trauma of the moment, Alan hadn't recognised Maria. Presumably they had both been at Lisa and Graham's wedding — but how memorable would that be? A brief meeting, if that, quickly forgotten.

No, she would make sure this was all right. If she arranged to meet Maria in the pub, somewhere neutral, answered her questions as best she could and satisfied Maria's feeling of frustration, it would all be resolved. No doubt Alan would meet Maria eventually, with Birkedge being a smallish village — but by then she would no longer be a threat to his peace of mind. Jen was determined of that.

When Alan went into the kitchen to make coffee, Jen quickly tidied the desk as best she could and slid Lisa's photograph back into the drawer. Some other time.

5

Dorothy would never have believed that Martonby Hall, which had always seemed so aloof, could have become such a friendly and familiar place. That first day, she drove home wondering how she had dared, how had she found the courage? There was a re-run of everything Frank had said sliding around in her brain. She was almost too elated to see straight.

The phone was ringing as Dorothy reached the front door and she ran to pick it up. 'Oh, Frank! Hello!' She knew that delight was making her voice squeak.

'I've got in touch with my solicitor, a very good man. Would you like me to run you over to see him? He could fit you in this afternoon as it happens.'

She was still breathing too quickly. 'I'm so sorry, I can't. I have to be back here for the boys coming home.' Disappointment swept through her but the boys' needs had to come first.

'Tomorrow morning? Ten o'clock.'

Once again, the relief was leaving her legs weak. 'Oh, yes. That would be fine.'

He laughed. 'Don't worry, I wasn't going to be put off that easily.'

How was it he understood her so well? And when Malcolm, who had been married to her for more than fifteen years, had never known who she was. She had been a fool to fall for Malcolm so quickly. She must have been a very poor judge of character, she thought but she would never make that mistake again.

The session with Frank's solicitor was swift, efficient and satisfactory. Ernest Barnes was balding, with glasses, and reminded Dorothy of her own father. But her father had never paid much attention to her, let alone treated her with deference. 'Leave this with me,' Ernest Barnes said. 'Don't worry about a thing. Everything will be arranged to your advantage.'

She shook his hand and left his office feeling more relaxed than she had in days. And Frank was sitting downstairs in the reception area with the *Telegraph*. 'Would you care to join me for lunch?'

Dorothy nodded, as if lunch with an attractive man was an everyday thing. 'That would be lovely. Thank you.'

She chose Chicken Marengo because it sounded exotic and Frank paid her the compliment of saying that he would have the same. 'An excellent choice.' They discussed food and restaurants in general for a few moments, before he continued, 'You must be very fond of your house, Dorothy, to put up such a fight for it.'

'I am. I loved it from the first. I think that's why Mrs Laurence let us have it and lowered her price. We could never have afforded anywhere so lovely otherwise, even with the money my grandparents left me.' She smiled. 'They were very cautious. It only became available to me on my marriage.'

Frank nodded. 'Ah, I understand. That explains a great deal.'

She was surprised for a moment, wondering why he was looking so solemn. 'Oh, no. It was nothing like that. Malcolm didn't know about the money at first. No, we were both very much in love. It was all very romantic.'

'I'll take your word for it. But I expect you would think the best of anyone, even the blackest villain.'

Dorothy thought about that too. 'I do try to see the best in people. I prefer doing that. It gives you a happier view of life.'

Frank smiled. 'I hope you'll succeed in seeing my better side.'

'But that's easy. I hardly have to try at all.' She blushed. 'I'm sorry, that sounds girlish and silly.'

'Never that. And I'm grateful for your vote of confidence in an ageing businessman with an anti-social son, an absentee, career-conscious daughter and a crumbling mansion. As parents, I suspect we have more power and influence than we ever dream of. Do you ever think that? But of course, your influence is for nothing but good.'

Dorothy shuddered, thinking of Malcolm and the pet rabbit and the severity of his punishments, such as shutting the boys in dark outhouses for an hour or more. With her love, she could help her boys forget. She must undo any possible harm. 'I do hope so. I don't want them to remember the unpleasant things.' And she wanted to talk about Malcolm's right to see his sons. This was worrying her now and she should have asked the solicitor about it.

Frank, however, was patting her hand and looking serious once more. 'I can understand your feelings. Might it be better to remove them from those painful surroundings and make a completely new start?'

She was shaking her head before he finished the sentence. 'No, no. They love that house as I do. The boys and I will never leave Sellybrook, Frank, believe me. Never.'

'Of course, of course. You're absolutely right. I was merely exploring all the possibilities and getting to grips with the situation.'

She chuckled. 'I forgive you. I know you have my best interests at heart.'

'I've enjoyed your company so much today, Dorothy. For a couple of hours, I forgot my loneliness and took pleasure in our conversation. You can have no idea how much that has meant to me.'

She whispered, 'Oh, Frank.' Because yes, she knew how he felt and she felt exactly the same but it was too soon, wasn't it, to tell him so? And the boys were another consideration. She must introduce Frank to them very, very carefully but at last it seemed as if a future of happiness lay before her.

She would grasp one day at a time.

* * *

Jen was expecting Maria to get in touch by phone, if she had given it much thought at all. And Alan had been out all afternoon, doing some property viewings. He had only been in five minutes when the bell rang. But here was Maria, folder in hand, smiling a greeting and confident of her welcome, moving forwards before Jen could think of how to stop her.

'Alan's in,' she said, stupidly. Because surely Maria had intended coming round when he was out? If they were going to have this discussion about Lisa.

'I hoped he would be. I thought I would apologise again and enquire after your sweet little cat.'

'He's in the shower.' Jen was getting a grip of it now. 'I'll pass on the message. I'm not sure this is a good time for discussing the outing. My mother's here as you know and we'll be eating shortly.'

'I'm so sorry. When you're on your own and always busy, busy, busy

— well, I just eat on the go. I forget other people prefer to be conventional and domesticated.' She didn't sound sorry at all. 'But it will only take five minutes, tops. Better get the ball rolling, hadn't we? Or Harold will be after us.'

The sooner they started, the sooner she would be gone, Jen reasoned. And now Maria, who had obviously been prepared for this and ready to overcome any objections, was sailing into the sitting room and greeting Erica like a long-lost friend. Jen could hardly throw her out. She didn't offer a drink. That would only slow things down. 'And you've just done this up? Lovely. Interesting that you've left that wall. I tend to go for as much space as possible. Light and air every time.'

'We removed a couple. It's given us a good-sized kitchen diner.' Perhaps even now, Alan might not remember Maria from Graham and Lisa's wedding. If Jen intercepted him on the stairs, he could avoid the sitting room altogether.

That might work. She was hardly concentrating as Maria cheerfully displayed two A4 sheets detailing all the places already visited. 'Oh, dear.' She brought herself back to the task in hand and read the busy pages with dismay. 'Is there anywhere you haven't been?'

Maria swayed backwards as she laughed. 'My problem exactly. They're a very active bunch.'

'Well, leave it with me. Being new to the area, as you know, I'll have to look them up. Find them all on the map.'

'I have a map here. And I do think it would be best if we could possibly come to a decision now.'

Jen stared at her. 'I don't see how that would be possible. Unless you've had further thoughts about this yourself.' She felt as if she was taking part in a play where only one of the actors knew the script. As if she were performing to some complex plan Maria had thought up. Why on earth had Maria bothered to involve someone else at all if that was the case?

'Yes — as a matter of fact, I've had a bit of an inspiration.'

'How nice.'

'We've been to everywhere open to the public — but what about approaching some of the old houses that are privately owned? There are some beautiful old places well within driving distance.'

Jen frowned. 'I can't see the owners being too keen on that idea.'

'In return for a fee? Cash in hand?'

'They'd be wanting more than we could afford, surely? And which houses in particular did you have in mind? Excuse me, that will be Alan now. I'll just enlist his help in the kitchen and then I can get back to you.'

Alan was halfway down the stairs. She said, 'I won't be long but somebody from the local history society's popped round. If you could go and do a bit of stirring, open the wine — I'll get rid of her as soon as I can.'

Directly behind her, Maria said, 'Hello, Alan.'

Jen's head snapped round. Maria was smiling but Jen could feel the tension. Alan's knuckles were white as his hand tightened on the banister rail but his voice was calm. 'Hello, Maria.'

Jen looked from one to the other. It was more than tension. There was a long moment of silence, where their expressions did not alter but Jen felt as if some kind of electric message were passing between them, excluding her.

Alan said, 'I didn't recognise you yesterday. Not at first. Your hair's different, isn't it? And it was a very long time ago.'

'It was. I have to come clean. I already knew yesterday, but then I had that stupid accident with your cat.' Maria spread her hands disarmingly. 'It hardly seemed the right time to be introducing myself.'

'Of course. Understandable.'

Jen stepped back. 'Shall we go and sit down?' Her voice was tight and controlled. She only wanted to push Maria out of the front door and away but that would hardly be civilised. And wouldn't solve anything. Maria was already returning to the sitting room ahead of her. 'And I'm afraid I've known who you were for a few weeks now. You e-mailed our office for house specs, Alan, and I put two and two together. I made sure I sent you some very high-quality specifications where I knew the vendors would be open to negotiation. I dealt with your request personally.'

'And very efficiently,' Alan said politely. 'But the name?'

'I kept my ex-husband's name, as it happened. I hoped it would eventually be a pleasant surprise.'

'Yes.'

Jen was trying to piece all this together. So if Alan had been trying to escape Maria's calls about Lisa, he had unwittingly taken the very worst course of action. Thinking he was leaving his tormentor behind in

London. And presumably he would have emailed various online agencies with his requirements in the first place. All too easy for Maria to respond. And with the very best advice.

But there was something else. A very long time ago? She felt as if she was breathing inside a balloon. 'So you two already know each other?' Even before Lisa and Graham.

'Yes,' Alan said. 'Or we did. We were at university together.'

Maria was chatting on, smiling. 'And I'm sorry, Alan, to be landing Jen with this mammoth task.' She picked up her list and wafted it in front of him as he sat down on the sofa, on the edge of the cushions. 'Jen has very kindly volunteered to organise our September trip. Particularly finding somewhere to go. The organisation is no problem, it practically organises itself. It's finding the destination that's difficult. We've had so many outings, we've been everywhere open to the public. But

Harold was so disappointed when I suggested we might have to repeat. That's what made me think twice about doing it again.'

'So why didn't you resign and have done with it?' Erica said. It was a wonder she had kept quiet for so long, Jen thought. 'I can't think of anything worse than being on a committee with Harold.'

Maria pulled a face. 'You're absolutely right. But Harold gave me the impression that he could be helpful, in all kinds of ways. That was before he retired, of course. And I can't say too much about it but there were times when things went much more smoothly for certain clients than I could have hoped.'

Jen stared at her. Surely Harold was incorruptible? 'Harold? I got the impression he would always be very correct.'

'As a general rule. But people are not always what they seem, are they?' She flashed Alan a knowing smile.

'And he's still promising to be helpful in various ways, although planning is all different now. I can't say any more, of course — ' She nodded, as if agreeing with herself.

Jen wasn't convinced. But whether Harold might be useful or not was hardly contributing to the present challenge. She sighed. 'It would be a shame to let them down, wouldn't it? I can see that. Helen's lovely and they all seem so keen.'

'Exactly.' Maria patted Jen's arm in that irritating way she had. 'I was just saying to Jen, Alan, that I thought we might try approaching the owners of old and interesting private houses? I'm sure there must be a number of those that would be suitable.' She paused, again looking directly at Alan.

'So do we know anyone who owns a big old house?' Erica said helpfully.

The name hung in the air between them, with no one actually saying it. Alan folded his arms. Jen said, 'If you mean Sellybrook, I don't think that would do at all.'

'Sellybrook! Of course,' Maria cried. 'That would be ideal. Just the right size and packed full of history.'

This was what she had been aiming at all along, wasn't it? Jen felt she had been manipulated and that Maria hadn't even troubled to be subtle about it. She said firmly, 'No. Graham's still living there. It would be intrusive.'

'Ah, that will explain why I haven't been able to contact him,' Maria said. 'I thought he was still working in Birmingham.'

Alan said suddenly, 'He left. Sold up. Too many unhappy memories, he said. And there was no need to stay when he took early retirement, health reasons or something. But living at Sellybrook isn't a permanent arrangement for him. It's only until he finds somewhere else to live.' He was tapping a hand on the sofa arm. 'Oh, what the hell. You have to go somewhere. Why not there? If it will help Jen out.'

Maria stood up. 'That's wonderful.

Thank you so much. We can really get on now.' She looked at her watch. 'Goodness, I won't take up any more of your time. If we could get together tomorrow evening, Jen, and finalise the details?' She raised her eyebrows, leaving Jen in no doubt as to the real reason for the discussion. 'You can come to mine.'

Jen followed her to the front door. Inside, she was seething. 'Thanks for landing me with this bombshell,' she hissed. 'You've set me up, haven't you? This was what you wanted all along.'

'How very melodramatic! It isn't like that at all. But I'll explain everything tomorrow when we can talk properly. Just opposite the pub on the village street, the new house standing alone. High Fields — name on the gate. Anytime after seven. Bye then.'

Alan had taken refuge in the kitchen, and was taking the casserole dish out of the oven. Jen took plates and cutlery from the cupboards and drawers. She said quietly, conscious of Erica but

101

unable to wait any longer, 'You never told me you knew Maria before.' She tried not to sound as if she was accusing him of anything, but the words were pouring out. 'You must have known before today. You must have recognised her voice when she kept phoning us. And you must have known the woman who was Lisa's cousin was the girl you knew. And she was more than just a friend, wasn't she?' She glanced over her shoulder, half expecting her mother to be right behind her, not wanting to miss anything. But Erica was over by the window, staring thoughtfully out at the garden.

Alan smiled at her. 'Phew, that's a lot of questions. But there's nothing for you to worry about. Trust me on that. Yes, she's an ex-girlfriend. Very ex. Anything there was between us is so far in the past I can hardly remember it.'

The plates stuttered in Jen's hands. She clattered them onto the table.

He was saying, 'I didn't realise at first. I didn't know she lived here. I didn't know she ran an estate agency, and that the very helpful person handling our queries would turn out to be her. She's engineered this herself for some reason. You saw what she's like.'

Jen opened her mouth to admit that she did know the reason and then changed her mind and said only, 'Yes. Very determined. She couldn't have known we would choose this house or even this village. Though I suppose the package from this area did have the best bargains.'

'It wouldn't have made any difference. If that hadn't worked, she would have found something else. It's how she is.'

Just as long as one of Maria's targets, apart from discovering the truth about Lisa, didn't turn out to be retrieving Alan. But none of this was his fault. 'Never mind. These things happen. Life's full of coincidences.' She paused. No, she had to ask. 'Except — Alan, why is there a picture of Lisa in the desk drawer?'

His face went blank. 'Desk drawer? I didn't know it was there. I didn't know I still had that photo. I think I'll sprinkle some basil leaves on the top of this.'

'I wondered why you had it at all.'

He turned, basil leaves from the herb pot in his hand, and took her by the shoulders. 'Look, Jen, Lisa died before I met you. Forget it. Kiss me.'

It wasn't an answer but she laughed and obeyed and a gust of wind sent the kitchen door swinging behind them. She felt loved and reassured. He was right and she was being foolish and insecure. She felt much happier as they sat down at the table.

'Sellybrook,' her mother said. 'I was about to suggest it myself. It was quite obvious that woman wouldn't leave us in peace until somebody did.'

Jen passed her the salad. 'I didn't know you knew anything about it.' Erica had always been hinting that they didn't know enough about Alan's family background. Surely she hadn't been checking him out? Jen went cold, imagining Erica calling in a private investigator. She wouldn't put it past her.

'Ah, you see.' Erica waved her fork, obviously pleased to be surprising her daughter. 'My old friend Mary Tattersall moved to Martonby in Lancashire when her husband died.' She smiled knowingly. 'And she soon found out about the house and who it had belonged to, and when you met Alan, she put two and two together.'

She would, wouldn't she? Any friend of Erica's would do just that. 'And you never said a word about it.' But that was so like her mother, Jen thought. Collecting and savouring the snippets of knowledge. Waiting for just the right moment to release them, for maximum effect.

'Mary's in Australia with her son at present. And I don't like to gossip, dear.'

'We won't start now in that case. Your chicken will be cold. Were you going to get on with the garden tonight, Alan?'

He was — they agreed that with the house finished, they must turn their attention outside before even thinking about putting it on the market. Erica exclaimed, surely they wouldn't be moving again? And they explained their plan of living in one property while doing up the next. This distracted her nicely as she didn't approve.

Jen set the dishwasher going and followed Alan outside, needing to talk to him alone. 'We don't have to visit Sellybrook if you don't want to. I could find somewhere else, I'm sure.' He had never suggested going to see Graham or the house since moving here, even though it could be little more than an hour's drive away.

He was whistling to himself. 'No, it's OK. I was thinking it over while we were eating. I don't mind. I would have had to make contact with him when we sell it, anyway. That house is half mine and an unfulfilled asset.'

'Oh. Do you think Graham's had

enough time?' So weary and ill when they had last seen him. He needed to rest and recover.

'It was only ever a temporary measure for him. He's always known that. The trouble with Graham is that he'll let things drag on and on without making any effort to find anywhere else. Unless I give him a bit of a push.'

'You won't expect him to leave in a hurry, will you? That doesn't seem too fair.'

'Of course not. But it's time we got rid of it. I'm glad this outing has come up; it's given me a push too. Needed to be done. We should have sold it years ago.'

'I suppose so,' Jen said doubtfully.

'Don't worry, Graham will come round. He'll agree with me. He always does. And about the outing — I'll ring him now.' He took his phone out of his pocket. 'Have you a date? A choice of dates? That's fine. Oh, hi Graham. How are you? It's Alan. Yes, I know. Been meaning to get in touch since we moved. Yes, we're up in Yorkshire now.'

His voice was pleasant and cheerful. No sign of any problem between them. No hint that it had been a very long time since they had last spoken. 'I'll tell you what it is. I've been approached by our local history group, wanting to have a day out to Sellybrook.'

She was listening intently, trying to catch anything, even a tone of voice from the other end. Impossible. She was only left with Alan's half of the conversation but which seemed to be going well. 'Yes, that's perfect. And yes, that's a good idea. In fact I think Jen mentioned something of the sort. Jen, if we could go over one day beforehand, to discuss the arrangements, plan the tour? Yes, that's great.'

Jen's tension dispersed. Thank goodness for that. She had hardly dared to hope that Graham would be so helpful and receptive. They hadn't even needed to ask for a preparatory visit; that suggestion had come from him.

But would he be so helpful once he

realised that his time at Sellybrook was strictly limited? Jen hoped Alan knew what he was doing. But he had grown up with Graham and Jen hardly knew him at all, although on the very few occasions they had met, he had seemed so vulnerable. Still, it made sense. She heard a sound from the back door and turned to see her mother beckoning, with a look of importance on her face. Sighing, she went in, closing the back door behind her.

'I've just remembered.' Erica screwed up her eyes. 'Something else Mary Tattersall told me. I think you should ask Alan to tell you what happened to his mother.'

6

You would have thought Frank had always been part of their lives. The boys were given the run of the hall grounds when Simon Parkestone was away at Oxford, and that was wonderful, although most of the estate had to be off limits during the long vacations. 'He relishes the shooting when he comes home,' Frank explained, apologetically. 'And we wouldn't want any accidents. Easy to make a mistake in the heat of the moment.'

And how well Frank understood her boys. Right from the start, he seemed to know that distraction was the best way to handle Alan, and that Graham was always happy to join in. Football was followed by something called a Bullworker that Graham had mentioned, and a set of oil paints. All these things and more had been tried, wearied of and cast aside by Simon — or so Frank said.

Dorothy shook her head, smiling. They were watching them trying out the swingball set on the lawn. 'You do too much for them.'

'I'm glad to. Your two are so appreciative. I'm very fond of them. Even Graham is coming out of himself now that he's more used to me. Not like Simon, such an odd, morose sort of fish.'

'He's not so bad,' Dorothy said quickly although it was indeed very difficult to warm to Simon. 'No son of yours could be all bad. He's just a bit abrupt sometimes, but that can be a form of shyness, can't it? I'm sure he'll grow out of it. And he's certainly coming out of his shell with the boys. Graham told me he sometimes joins in when they're kicking a football around in the paddock. And even helps him with his plant collection.'

'Does he? That is a surprise.' Frank shook his head. 'I can hardly get two words out of him. And his sister hasn't much time for him either, never had. But then, there's quite an age gap between them. And as you know, Samantha has very little time for anything relating to home and family these days. Too busy jetting around the world, doing deals.'

'You must be very proud of her.'

'Oh, I am, of course. I would just like to see her sometimes, that's all. All I get is the occasional and very rushed phone call. Usually when she's waiting to board a plane and has nothing else to do. I told you, didn't I, that she's acquired a wealthy fiancé now? But there's been no mention of introducing him to Simon and myself.'

'There will be. Don't worry.' She loved being able to reassure him like this, her turn at last to do something useful for him.

His voice became softer. 'And you know, I should very much like to introduce her to you. I think you know why.'

112

Dorothy was wary at once, unable to stop herself shivering away like a frightened fawn. 'There's no need to hurry as far as I'm concerned. I'm happy just as we are. Really.' It was too soon for anything else. She didn't want this.

He began gently stroking her arm in the mushroom-coloured cardigan, not even touching her skin. 'It's all right. It's all right. Nothing will change. No one will rush you.'

'All I want is to be happy and safe, with my sons.'

'That's what I want for you too. All I ask is that you let me be here for you.'

Dorothy made herself smile. 'I don't know where we would be without you.' But there was a tight ball of panic below her ribs. What was he asking exactly? She didn't want anything to change. There had been too much change in her life. She wanted calm, the quiet of the stilled pool in the woodland where she was learning to sit and experience true peace. She needed more time yet, more healing. She said, 'Having your friendship is very important to me.'

He was nodding. 'I understand.' His fingers moved down towards her hand, paused, moved away. 'I would never dream of altering the balance we enjoy. Not unless you wanted anything to alter.'

Yet part of her did crave the security Frank could offer. She didn't understand herself. The boys, she thought, I must think of the boys. I'm right about that.

But soon that excuse was to be whipped from under her feet. There was one half-term in particular that she would always remember. Alan was bolting cornflakes, splashing milk onto the breakfast table while Graham was spreading jam and honey on his toast, half a slice each. He moved his knife with control, measuring a line across the butter and separating the two toppings with care.

Dorothy tutted a little and fetched

the dishcloth. 'So what's today's hurry, Alan?'

'Oh, I'm going on a bike ride with Nails. Stephen Naylor.' He would probably end up doing something completely different.

'And what are your plans, Graham?' She must not leave him out of the conversation but she knew what he would say.

'Nothing much. Some reading. Are you going anywhere, Mum?'

'No, Frank has a meeting. And I wouldn't leave you here on your own.'

Alan was in and out of the dining room, looking for his anorak. 'Gray's old enough now, Mum. He doesn't mind.' Now he was back at the table, blobbing jam onto his toast. 'Mum, why don't you marry Frank?'

'Butter, Alan? It is the best butter.' She knew that her laugh, quoting the Mad Hatter's Tea Party, was high and squeaky.

'I'm not bothered, thanks. Come on, what's putting you off?'

'Oh, well.' She put a hand to the silver pendant round her neck, Frank's birthday gift. 'I have you two to think of.'

Graham cut along his dividing line and cut each half into several pieces, trimming and honing each one until they matched up to some unexplained standard of his own. Alan said, 'I don't see why. Anyway, we like him. It would make sense all round. Wouldn't it, Graham?'

Graham nodded. He had arranged his toast pieces in an alternating sequence and was beginning by eating a honey one.

'There's the house, you know,' Dorothy said.

'Well, we like it here but we won't be living here for ever, will we, Gray?' Alan said. Graham looked doubtful. 'Anyway, first point, your happiness is more important. Second point, that solicitor of Frank's would sort things out with Dad. Third point, Frank could probably afford to buy it outright off Dad. QED. Have to rush, bye.'

Dorothy looked after him through the empty doorway. Her well-constructed objections had been knocked to pieces. Graham put his current piece of jam toast down and went to shut the door. 'There you are, Mum.'

'What? Oh, thanks.' She shook her head, trying to clear her thinking. 'I never thought — are you sure you wouldn't mind? Do you agree with Alan?'

'I usually do.'

'But this time?'

He nodded again. 'Yes.'

She spread her hands across the table, still damp from Alan's milk splashes. 'I didn't realise. I assumed I must keep things as they were for you — until you were grown up.'

'Alan is grown up.'

'Nearly, I suppose. Yes. But Graham, if I should marry Frank, you do know, don't you, that I will always love you and Alan?'

'Oh, yes. But Frank makes you happy. And he can look after you.

That's what I want for you, Mum. We both do. We worry about you. Would you like the last piece?'

She took it absently, eating it without looking at it.

'It's a honey one,' Graham said reproachfully.

'Oh, thank you. That was sweet of you. But you know, dear, Frank may not want to marry me.'

Graham looked at her and sighed. He seemed at that moment, far older and wiser than she was. 'Of course he does. And anyway, Mum, if you're worried about Frank having more money than us, I don't think he has.'

'What, with the Hall and his French holiday homes?' She laughed. 'Where did you get that idea?'

'Simon told me. He hears him on the phone, swearing in French.'

'Surely not.' The whole thing was impossible. Frank was always so generous. Simon must have misunderstood. Frank always said his son had no business sense. 'Besides, Frank never swears.'

'I suppose he doesn't. Not to us. But you will marry him, won't you?'

'I don't know.' She felt confused. She tried to be practical. 'If you're right about the money, Frank couldn't afford to buy your father's half of the house anyway. It wouldn't work. As it is, I can stay here until you're twenty-one whatever happens.'

'Mr Barnes would sort everything out for you.'

'He can't work miracles. And if Simon's right, if Frank does have any kind of financial problem, I couldn't possibly burden him with my muddled concerns. That wouldn't be fair. Oh, there's the post.' Dorothy picked it up and pulled a face as she recognised Malcolm's writing. Whatever it was, it wouldn't be good. She sat down to open it, frowning at the single sheet of paper. Was this a joke? Malcolm seemed to be relinquishing all claims to the house and thanking her for the generous settlement. What settlement? It made no sense at all. Perhaps he was taunting her but she couldn't see why. What could he possibly gain from this?

Perhaps it was part of some larger plan. It might explain other letters she had received from various bodies unknown to her over the past couple of weeks. There had been a development firm expressing an interest in buying the house, for instance, among others. All of them junk mail naturally and had gone straight in the bin. But now she thought that Malcolm might have instigated them somehow, to tempt her into selling. Just like him.

She phoned Malcolm's office. 'I don't understand this letter, Malcolm.'

'Ah, the letter.' He sounded unusually affable. 'Ask me no questions and I'll tell you no lies. Suffice it to say that I'm well satisfied. Very well satisfied. The tables are turning and my ship has come in. Far better than having that depressing old mausoleum hanging round my neck for evermore. What kind of an asset was that? No, you can't beat paper.'

She spoke clearly and firmly. 'Malcolm, I do not know what you are talking about.'

'You're not meant to know. But good grief, Dorothy, that new man of yours must be totally besotted to do a deal like this. And he calls himself a businessman?'

'You mean Frank Parkestone?'

His voice became harsh. 'I've said nothing. The letter was necessary, stipulated. Oh, and I want the boys to come over one weekend. I haven't seen them in months.'

'Of course you can see them. There's no question about that.' Well, she would put the letter in a safe place and perhaps Edward Barnes would advise her as to whether it was a legally acceptable document and where she stood.

But a small nugget of joy and gratitude was growing inside her. She so wanted to believe it. Her house would be safe. She would have no need to worry. At last. And all Frank's doing. Dear Frank.

Jen knew that she didn't want to do this. She felt she would be deceiving Alan somehow. The trip was one thing, this illicit discussion of Maria's suspicions a different matter altogether. She said cautiously, 'I'm going round to Maria's tonight, remember?'

He was engrossed in his laptop, pricing building materials. 'That's fine.'

Hardly the response of a guilty lover and Alan always spoke without thinking. He would be hopeless at any kind of subterfuge. And now she had to concentrate on answering — or maybe fending off — Maria's questions about Lisa. Best to begin with an attack.

Almost before sitting down in Maria's incredibly spacious and well-designed ground floor room, Jen launched into telling Maria everything relevant. From when she had pulled up at the taped-off bridge to Alan rushing off in answer to Graham's phone call the next morning. Maria heard her out, taking occasional notes which was a bit off-putting and then asked her to repeat the conversation Jen had first overheard between Alan and Graham.

Jen sat back. 'There you are. Perhaps knowing all these details will help you to come to terms with your cousin's death. I do hope so. This must have been very difficult for you.'

'What?' Maria was staring beyond her without seeing her. 'Sorry? Oh, I get it. You think this has been some kind of impromptu therapy session.'

Jen frowned. 'What else would it be? I wanted to help you.'

'No, I'm afraid not. I'm quite capable of sorting out my own hang-ups, thank you.' Maria leaned forward. 'I'm not convinced that Lisa committed suicide.' She was nodding, her voice cool and determined.

'Sorry?'

'Someone killed her.'

Jen laughed. The suggestion was ludicrous. 'But if the police are satisfied, I don't see — '

'The police are a waste of time. I've been to them, naturally, but no one would listen. They think I'm as unstable as poor Lisa obviously was. No, I'll have to have much more to present to them before they'll pay any attention.'

Anger was blossoming and Jen didn't try to stop it. The anger was blocking the uneasy, crawling sensation beneath her ribs. 'No doubt this is why you've manipulated Alan and me into suggesting Graham's present home for this outing of yours. I expect Graham's refusing to talk to you and you've come up with this devious way of getting at him.'

'And having a good look round the house. Exactly. You're very sharp, Jen. We can work well together.'

'This is unreal. I've no intention of helping you with this mad idea.'

Maria's eyes were wide as she smiled. 'I'm quite prepared to go it alone as far as my suspicions are concerned. That needn't have anything to do with you. Just get me there and I'll have the opportunity I need. Coffee?'

Jen was thinking quickly. Her first instinct had been to cancel the whole thing. She was so furious at being played with like this. But if so, what would Maria do next? And Maria's suspicions must be merely the product of excessive grief and denial and would easily prove to be unfounded, wouldn't they? Perhaps it would be safer to allow her to have her way, in a supervised situation. She said, slowly, as Maria produced mugs and home-baked biscuits, 'And if you find nothing, that will be the end of it? Your fears will be laid to rest?'

'Of course. Believe me, Jen, I don't want to be proved right. It's just that there are so many details that don't add up for me.'

A deeper and unwelcome knowledge somewhere within Jen stirred itself. She said lightly, 'I suppose Graham is your prime suspect? The husband usually is.'

Maria hesitated for the first time. 'Yes. That's right.'

Jen shook her head. 'I didn't mean that seriously, Maria. I've read somewhere that most murders are committed by a relative, that's all. What possible reason could you have for suspecting poor Graham of something like that?'

Maria shrugged. 'As you say, he was the husband and had the opportunity. And there was no love lost between them by then. Besides, he was always so quiet. You never knew what he was thinking.'

Jen's shoulders relaxed with relief. So there was nothing concrete or even sensible behind all this. 'I think I have to agree with the police reaction. You don't seem to have much to go on. You can hardly accuse someone because they're too quiet.'

'Someone killed her, Jen. I knew Lisa and so did you. She would never have killed herself. Empty threats, yes, because she could be a bit of a drama queen on occasion. But that's all they would be. Empty.'

Jen didn't like the new turn the

conversation was taking. It was the one bit of logical deduction she could not disagree with. 'Everyone can act out of character sometimes. Which of us really knows anyone else? Really knows them?' She had a sudden unwanted image, seeing herself replacing that photograph in the desk drawer. She said briskly, 'So you'll be wanting to come on my initial visit to Sellybrook, when I go to check facilities, timings et cetera?'

'There, I knew you were the right person for this. You'll have everything under control. And usually, yes, I would be coming. But no, thanks. Not much opportunity to slip away and I'd only be arousing Graham's suspicions.'

Jen set her mug down, briskly. 'Thanks a lot. You don't seem worried that I shall be on my own with a suspected murderer for a couple of hours.'

Maria laughed. 'Honestly, if Graham killed Lisa — and even I can see it's open to doubt — it will have been after a row, in the heat of the moment. No one else is in any danger. But I need to find out. Lisa deserves that much, doesn't she?'

Jen sighed. 'Yes. All right. And Alan will be with me. And I'll even give you my full opinion of Graham and how he conducts himself and whether I think he would be capable of anything like that. But don't expect me to go round rootling for clues.'

Maria seemed disappointed but she only said, 'Fair enough. And thanks, Jen. This means so much to me. You have to go? Well, we'll keep in touch.' She followed Jen across the light-filled, amazing space to the front door. 'You knew, didn't you, that Alan had an affair with Lisa? Before she died?'

A person who suddenly wasn't Jen nodded somehow. Keeping her face straight was painful as glands below her ears twinged with the effort. 'Oh, yes. He told me everything.'

And she had known without admitting it to herself. As soon as she had found that all-too-recent photograph.

Somehow she got herself out of Maria's house without giving herself away. Or she hoped she had. She was walking mechanically, hardly aware of where she was going.

What was she going to do? There was no choice. She knew she had to tackle Alan about this. Now, tonight, before she lost the courage. Fortunately Alan was out in the garden, making a start on dismantling the old garden shed, so there was no need to try and avoid her mother. He had a large hammer in one hand. Wood was splintering and crashing onto the path.

Jen said, 'Maria has just told me that you had an affair with Lisa.'

He paused, wiping his forehead with his sleeve but without any sign of surprise. 'I suppose I should have told you. It's not something I'm proud of. It just happened. I bumped into her at a conference. She was on a course. We were in the same hotel.'

She felt ashamed of herself for prying because this was in his past and it was foolish to be demanding the information like this. But Maria had left her no alternative. 'Did Graham know?'

'I hope not. I don't think so.' He threw the hammer down with the wood. The thump of it hitting the concrete reverberated through her head. He folded his dusty arms round her. 'Listen, Jen, I didn't want to upset you and I knew it would. It only lasted a few weeks. I soon remembered why I'd found Lisa so annoying in the first place. Forgive me?'

'Silly. There's nothing for me to forgive. I didn't know you then.' She hesitated. 'Graham, perhaps — but if he doesn't know, there's no need for him to find out, is there?' She remembered that conversation at Pamela's wedding. No wonder Alan had asked Graham if Lisa had been having an affair. He wanted to discover whether Graham knew about it. And also she should tell Alan what Maria had said about Graham. She rehearsed the words in her mind: Maria seems to think that

Graham might have killed Lisa. I told her that was a terrible thing to say.

The words died. What was the point? Alan would be devastated. There was no reason to pass on Maria's misguided poison. Or for Alan to be involved in any of this at all. She said, 'You don't have to come on this outing if you don't want to. I know it could be awkward for you.' He didn't say anything and she blundered on, with her mother's snippet of gossip still hovering unwanted in her mind. 'I know that house will hold sad memories for you. Of both your parents and your mother in particular, I'm sure.' She paused. Alan was stooping to put a pile of old plant pots into a bin bag. And now she was definitely prying and hated herself but couldn't stop. 'If you ever want to talk about your mother, I'm here for you, Alan.'

'I know.' He dropped the pots and took her in his arms again, holding her tightly so she couldn't see his face. 'I don't feel I want to talk about it, even after all this time. You see, my mother committed suicide too and when Lisa did the same, it brought everything back. That's why I can't bear to talk about her either. Or even to think about it.'

Jen could have wept. 'Alan, I'm so sorry. I should never have mentioned it.' What on earth had Erica been playing at, with her silly little hints?

'That's OK. And having you has helped me so much. I would never have got over the circumstances of Lisa's death without you.' He was breathing quickly, harsh rasping breaths. 'If I talk to anyone, it will be you. One day, perhaps.'

7

Driving over to Martonby for her afternoon of checking and planning, Jen found the lane leading to Sellybrook and the Hall without any trouble. Alan had discovered an urgent appointment and she hadn't pressed him. Erica had been only too willing to come instead.

Here was the driveway Alan had described with an unusual rocky hillock to the left. Jen said, turning in, 'This must be it. And can you leave Graham to me, please, Mother?'

'Don't worry. I shall only speak when spoken to. I know how to behave.'

Trees on one side of the drive along the stream and on the other side the rough ground beyond the hillock gave way to more trees until they were driving through a green tunnel. They came out of it abruptly and the house was long and low and solid, with old chimneys and mullion windows. 'It's perfect,' Jen said. 'Alan never told me how beautiful it was.'

'Damp and unhealthy,' Erica pronounced. 'You can tell by the number of willows. They prefer marshy ground.' She hopped out of the car like a teenager. Graham was waiting at the front door to greet them, smiling. The edginess had gone. Now he was calm and still, much more relaxed than Alan.

Jen smiled. 'It's Graham, isn't it? I'm Jen, Alan's wife. We have met before, briefly.' Leave it at that. Don't remind him of Lisa and the wedding and the inquest. She brushed her hair back, something she always did when she was nervous. She brought her hands down, quickly. 'And this is my mother, Erica. I'm sorry that Alan isn't here. The solicitor needed to see him at the last minute. We're into property developing, you see. A new venture. Something came up with one of our purchases. One of those last-minute glitches. You know how it is.' She knew she was explaining too fully. Too much and too fast.

Graham waited politely until she ran out of steam. She couldn't tell whether he was disappointed. 'Never mind. These things happen. And especially to Alan. Do come in. Sorry about the weather; I don't know if we'll be able to get round the grounds today. Unless you've brought wellies and water-proofs.'

'It doesn't matter. Just as long as we can get an idea.'

'And you're bringing a coach load of historians to look round the house. I'm flattered, believe me. I only hope the house and I can match up to your expectations.'

'That's why we've come today. I need to estimate timings and evaluate subject matter and work out whether we need to move on somewhere else after lunch.'

'Easily solved. There's the Hall next door if necessary. Not quite as old as this but mainly eighteenth century all the same. I'm sure Simon Parkestone wouldn't object, not if I ask him. The grounds are extensive, even without the portions that have been sold off for the housing estate and the golf course. And one piece of land used to belong to this house until comparatively recently. That's something your historians might find interesting.'

'That would be great.' Jen was beginning to relax. The tranquillity of the house and surrounding woodland were seeping through. This must be the secret of Graham's stillness. Maria's suspicions were making less and less sense and she would push them to the back of her mind. She couldn't imagine Graham laying a finger on anyone in anger.

He was saying, 'No trouble at all. Anything for Alan and his family. He and I may have been sadly lax at keeping in touch — you know how it is — but we'll always be there for each other. We both know that. And if this is a success, perhaps I could follow Alan's example and initiate a business venture myself. I could show interested parties round the house. By appointment only, of course.'

'But — ,' Jen began and stopped. She had almost blurted out that he would hardly be here long enough. Obviously he didn't know yet that Alan wanted to sell up. Her face was hot with guilt. Should she say something?

Graham didn't seem to have noticed the interruption. 'I've done extensive research over the years, into the history of the house. Purely for my own interest. But now I'm very pleased that I did.' His face was bright with pleasure at being able to help. Jen felt even worse. 'But don't be standing out here. We'll have a look round outside later, when this drizzle clears. Come in and have some coffee and I can show you some of my evidence — photographs, photocopies, books I've collected.'

Jen and Erica followed him inside and they stood in the dining room while Graham explained about the Parkestones, the family disputes over

137

the land with the Laurences who had lived at Sellybrook and the interpretations of various wills. Impossible not to respond to his enthusiasm. His speech quickened and his body language came alive.

'As you came through the central entrance hall, you would notice the traditional plan: the stairs straight ahead, this dining room to the left and the parlour to the right — going back to its original status as a large farmhouse. But I promised you coffee, not a lecture. Sorry, I get carried away.'

'No, that's fine. This is just what we need. I'm glad we came.'

They perched on a superb dark oak settle by the fireplace, its back forming a screen to the kitchen door. Graham was back in a few minutes with three mugs and Erica sipped and smiled. 'You can't beat a hot coffee on a cold damp day. I have only two vices, good strong coffee and chocolate.'

Graham smiled. 'You need a little vice, Erica, to achieve a balanced personality. My father used to say that chocolate was the ultimate symbol of decadence. We were never allowed to eat chocolate casually, only on special occasions and under supervision.'

'How long do you think a tour of the house would take, Graham?'

'As long as you like but I wouldn't want to overwhelm your group. How serious are they?'

'Very,' Jen said, thinking of Harold. 'Or some of them are. But I'm sure any bloodcurdling stories would go down well too.'

When Graham laughed, his eyes crinkled at the corners like Alan's. 'I'll see what I can do. The last Laurence heir was drowned accidentally, while playing in the pool in the woods, and then there's Celia Laurence who drowned herself after she was jilted. Actually, I have a painting in the parlour to show you which I like to think may be her. I paint myself and I copied it from one Simon Parkestone found in his attic, in very bad condition. It's the right period though.'

They followed him back across the stone-flagged hall. 'This is a large, cold area,' Erica said. 'Perhaps you could do with a rug.'

Graham's voice echoed across the flagstones. 'It's just as it was when we used to live here. The parlour is my favourite room.' He opened the white wooden door.

The impression was of brightness and light. Sunlight came and went as the clouds parted and the sunbeams glanced off the white painted panelling. What a contrast, Jen thought, to the darkness of the other rooms. A house of extremes.

'My mother's choice. Our tenants weren't allowed to alter a thing. I kept a careful eye on them.'

Jen went over to stand beside the white stone fireplace. 'And this is the painting of Celia? She looks so sad. I can imagine how she might have experienced some tragedy.'

Erica was at her shoulder. 'She looks

a bit like you, Jen. You have big, dark eyes.'

'I hope I don't look as mournful as that. Did you say you painted this, Graham? It's very good.'

'Yes, I'm quite pleased with that one although I'm only a copyist. I work from photographs usually. Wait a minute, I'll show you.' He went over to a cupboard set into the wall and almost hidden by one of the easy chairs. 'I did this one of Lisa.'

'Oh,' Jen said. Erica was raising her eyebrows behind Graham's back. Jen shook her head at her. They would just have to go with this. Anything else would seem impolite. Graham closed the cupboard and handed the small portrait to her, little more than A4 size. Jen studied it. Graham had a distinctive, detailed painting style that went beyond the photographic and the face was painfully real. Almost too real. 'But Graham, this is excellent. I do watercolours sometimes, flowers and things but I've never been any good at portraits.

Do you sell any?'

'It's only a hobby. I'm working on one of Simon Parkestone at present.' His eyes lit. 'I know, do you think Alan would like one of you? As a surprise gift?'

Jen didn't quite know what to say. 'I'm sure he'd love one. But what about the sittings?'

'No, no. I only need a couple of photographs. If you wait there, I can take them now.' Another cupboard and he produced a digital camera. 'Yes, that's fine. No, don't smile. Smiles tend to look false in a portrait.' His face was flushed.

All that stooping in low cupboards, Jen thought. 'You won't make me look sad though, like Celia? Alan says he loves me for my happy disposition.'

'I shall search for your true character and convey the personal. Celia has one of those universal faces. You can see many women that you know and have known in that gaze. Eternal woman-hood, contemplating the tragedies of life.'

Jen shivered. 'Could we do a specimen tour so that I can time it, if that's OK? Just to give me an idea.'

Again Graham spoke well, packing a lot of knowledge into a chatty, informal style as he explained everything, from the oldest features to the eighteenth- and early twentieth-century extensions.

They paused in silent surprise at the main bathroom at the top of the stairs, with its red and black squared floor and the single black wall, offsetting the other three, tiled in plain white. 'My father's creation, I'm afraid,' Graham said. 'He considered it a fine example of fifties contemporary.'

'You could have had it altered,' Erica said. 'I should, if I'd been your mother.'

'She kept it just as it was because it made Frank laugh,' Graham said. He was staring at the dimpled glass of the window. Sun and shadow glanced and dabbed onto the mirror over the washbasin. 'Frank Parkestone, Simon's father. Yes, I admired Frank. You should always make use of variation in circumstance to achieve your long-term aims, don't you think?'

'I expect so,' Jen said, not sure what to make of the remark.

Graham smiled, seeming to snap out of his moment of reverie and the tour continued successfully. By the time they had covered everything Jen could think of and she and Erica were getting back into the car, Jen was feeling actively positive about the outing. 'You can think what you like, Mother, but at last I know that volunteering myself wasn't a ghastly mistake. It's all going to work out.' And nothing to reinforce Maria's silly suspicions. She was even looking forward to it.

* * *

Unfortunately, the weekend that the boys would be staying with Malcolm, Frank had an unavoidable meeting in London. He was shaking his head in disappointment. 'And I don't like to think of you being alone in this house.

It's not something you're used to. It may be frightening for you.'

They were sitting in the warmth and fragrance of the herb garden where Graham had worked so hard to help her with laying the paths and the beds and then the planting. Eventually the lavender and sage would bush out over the mellow pink of the old bricks but already the bees were attracted to the tall spikes of foxgloves she had found growing wild and transplanted. In this small oasis of sunlight, such fears were nonsense. Dorothy laughed. 'No, no. I'm at my happiest when I'm here. This house and I belong together.'

'It's fine, I know, in the daylight when there are people here. But this house seems to attract sadness and solitude. Just think about all those creepy legends.'

'The boys made those up, Frank. Celia Laurence and the drowned boy heir never existed, poor tormented souls. Graham in particular has such a vivid imagination. I love to hear him telling those gruesome tales. He makes me laugh so much with the faces he pulls; you would almost think he believes them himself.'

'That sounds rather too blood-curdling for me. But I'm glad you can take it so lightly. Is there no one you could stay with? How about if I book you into a hotel? My treat.'

She spoke in a firm, strong voice. 'I shall be perfectly happy here. I'm even looking forward to it.' Although now Frank's concern was eating away at her so that she almost believed his fears — and when he was only trying to protect her, bless him.

He took both of her hands in his. 'I only want to look after you, Dorothy. If only we were married, there could be no question of a situation like this arising.'

She took her hands away. 'No, Frank. You turn everything into an opportunity but you know how I feel about that.' She was so happy just as they were. She woke each morning thankful for Frank and the boys and anticipating each day with pleasure. Two short days without them would be nothing amongst that jewel case of riches.

Dorothy waved Alan and Graham away on the first train on the Saturday morning and bought a pair of hiking socks and a book of easy walks as a birthday gift for Frank. They were always saying they would take up walking. 'One of these days,' they would say, laughing, though Dorothy teased that he would never actually go. So Frank would enjoy the joke even if they never used them. But they would, once the gift had been made. She would make sure of that. She bought paper and a matching label in the card shop too and went home well pleased with her purchases.

No need to garage the car as the weather was still warm and she would need to collect the boys again tomorrow. But now she was going to take the opportunity to paint the furniture in the boys' bedrooms. So you see, there was plenty to do.

She left the bedroom windows open to dispel the paint fumes and turned the radio on. Easy to work in Graham's ordered room but in Alan's, she had to heap the evidence of several long-neglected hobbies on his bed. Perhaps a clear-out would have been more appropriate. But wouldn't they be surprised when they came home — if they noticed? Well, Graham would notice. She chuckled to herself.

She cooked scrambled eggs on toast for a late tea. The dusk was warm and she left the curtains open to the friendly darkness of the garden as if the outside was another room. That way she felt part of the universe, knowing that the same sky caressed Alan and Graham — and Frank too. As the night deepened and the gently rustling leaves blended into the dark, however, she became conscious of being on view to the wildness out there. She closed the curtains and settled down to watch the TV. Perhaps there would be a decent play on.

The lights went out. The television gave a deep hiccup and she saw the white spot in the middle of the blank screen before that too disappeared and the darkness was absolute.

Oh, how annoying. Keep calm. Torches, matches, candles. Dorothy groped her way across to the settle and followed the back along to the kitchen door. This would be simple and straightforward because she had plenty of fuse wire in and knew what to do. There again, this might be a power cut and perhaps she should give Simon Parkestone a ring and check whether his electricity was off too.

Torch. Kitchen drawer.

Somewhere, a floorboard creaked. Dorothy stopped, her neck crawling.

Silly how sinister the ordinary noises made by the house had become. When you were on your own and in the dark. The sound came again. She knew all the noises the house made. The house was like a trusted friend. And this wasn't one of those cosy noises.

For a second or so, she was unable to move. But she had to move. She could hardly stand here in the kitchen doorway all night. She felt for the doorframe and made her feet follow her hands. Slowly, inch by inch and staring into the darkness, she felt her way along the kitchen surfaces to the drawer. She knew it wasn't far. Inches away. But what would she see when she switched the torch on? Don't think about that. It was something that had to be done. Don't think about the way the house itself was breathing round her.

I can't do this. Yes, you can.

First drawer. Second. Something danced and swung into her clutching fingers. Only the spider plant. Her hand slid beyond the plant saucer and touched something else, wet and furry. She jerked away and whatever it was leapt out onto the floor as if living, leaving a scent of animal earthiness hanging in the air. She squealed, unable to stop herself, found the right drawer, pulled it open and scrabbled inside. Yes, the torch was there and she switched it on, casting its beam across the room, banishing her fear in a swathe of light.

The furry thing was on the floor. A rabbit's paw, wet with blood. Horrible. She swallowed the sickness rising in her throat. It was dead. Nothing to fear there. There was blood on the white Formica and the drops spattered in a long trail across the cupboard door and the floor. What a mess. Well, she would leave that until the lights came on again but she could at least take a rag from her cleaning bucket, wrap it round the paw and throw the whole bundle into the bin. That was better.

She took a box of nightlights from the cupboard under the sink and lit one and then another. She was not going to leave this room dark if she had to return to see to the fuse box. And she had to get to the phone next. In the hall. Concentrate on that. Don't think about how the paw might have got there. Don't think about that at all.

Easier now that she had the torch. She paused to set nightlights in the dining room too. Little more than a glow but making a huge difference between sight and helplessness. She breathed slowly and deeply. She mustn't sound panicky when talking to Simon. Whatever would he think? And he would report back to his father that she wasn't capable of looking after herself without giving in to a cloud of neurotic fears. No.

She picked up the receiver and only realised, as there was no dialling tone, no sound, nothing, that the wire had been arranged neatly on top of the hall table. It had been cut through. She replaced the receiver quietly, although her hands were shaking. Her house keys and car keys were on the shelf by the phone where she always left them. Without thought, she picked them up and went out of the front door, still holding the torch and the nightlights

and matches. Very quietly and deliberately. So that the intruder could not
read her thoughts and predict her
actions. No use now to deny that there
was someone there. Inside. With her.
She locked the door behind her.
Nonsensical when the intruder was
inside already but this was a deeply
ingrained habit.

Thank goodness she hadn't put the
car away. Thank goodness. She slid the
key in the lock but the car door was
open already. Must have forgotten. She
pulled the door wide and the interior
light shone on the blood and fur on the
warm fabric of the driver's seat. She
screamed then, once, and threw the
rabbit carcase out onto the drive and
threw herself into the car, never caring
about the blood on her skirt and drove
like a mad thing down the drive,
thrusting through shadows, braking and
swerving.

And lights shone in her eyes as
another car edged through the gateway
towards her and she slammed both feet

down and flopped forward onto the wheel, pressing the horn and screaming.

The door was pulled open. A familiar voice. Strong, kind hands. 'Dorothy, Dorothy, stop, please. Whatever's the matter?'

And she had sworn that she wouldn't behave like this but she threw her arms around him, saying his name over and over again. 'Oh, Frank. Oh, Frank.'

8

Dorothy went back to Martonby Hall with Frank of course. His client had been called away unexpectedly so fortunately Frank had returned early. But he couldn't forgive himself for being absent when Dorothy had needed him most. No sign of the intruder now and no need to wonder how he had got in when the windows had been left open for the paint to dry. By now she was certain who had been responsible; it would be Malcolm. There was no doubt about that.

The following day, Frank proposed to her again. His most formal attempt yet and by the pool, now her favourite place. 'I used to come here to get away from Malcolm,' she told him as they strolled along the path through the wood. But she didn't want to think about Malcolm. Any thoughts of him were accompanied by a searing fury that made her head ache.

The sun was edging the dying leaves with shades of red and gold and the water around the rim of the pool reflected the light. Only the deeper water at the centre remained dark. And this was not a day for darkness. Dorothy felt light-headed as she took in greedy breaths of the frost-sharpened air. Here with Frank, she was strong at last. Anything was possible.

Frank took her hand. 'Please listen, Dorothy. I never wanted to hurry you but time is moving on and I'm older than you are. And I do so want to spend the rest of my life caring for you and your sons. I love you, Dorothy.'

Her emotions were tangled. Happiness began beneath her ribs and soared into her throat. She couldn't speak and squeezed his hand instead, nodding stupidly. But there was anger too and a determination not to be browbeaten into this. Malcolm would see an engagement as a sign of weakness and he would be right.

'Dorothy, will you marry me?'

'Yes, Frank. But not yet.'

He groaned. 'Oh, my sweet, stubborn, obstinate girl. What do I have to do? Surely after last night you must see that you need protection? You are so vulnerable here on your own, at the mercy of any random intruder.'

'That was no passing thief, Frank. No, that's what has made me so angry and so determined not to give in. To become engaged to you now would seem like running away.'

He was frowning at her. 'I don't know what you mean. All I know is that you need me as much as I need you.'

'But it was Malcolm, I knew it as soon as I saw the dead rabbit in the car. A reference to when he made our boys kill their pet rabbit just before he left us.'

'You think it was Malcolm?' He sighed. 'But the boys were with him.'

'Not all the time. He had to hurry off somewhere or so he said. He met them

157

off the train but then he told them he had something to do. And so he did because he had to drive up here, didn't he? Elizabeth took them out to a Wimpy Bar and to the pictures. Oh, they enjoyed themselves but they didn't see much of their father.' She stroked Frank's sleeve soothingly because he was breathing too quickly. 'Now you're angry too. I'm sorry, I didn't mean to tell you about this. There's no point in letting him upset both of us. And I shall marry you, Frank, of course I shall but I don't want Malcolm to think he has succeeded in frightening me and that I need any kind of protection from him.'

Frank sighed again. 'At least that's an acceptance of sorts. I suppose I must be satisfied with that. But please don't make me wait too long.'

'I just need a little more time. Only a little.' Fortunate that he hadn't seen what Malcolm had done to the birthday gift she had wrapped and labelled so carefully; the woollen socks stabbed and shredded with her nail scissors in a frenzy of jealousy.

'I had hoped — ' Frank hesitated and began again, as if making his mind up as he spoke. 'You see, I have to go away for a few days. A week maybe. I had hoped we could make our announcement before I left.'

'Oh, Frank! Have you?' The wave of disappointment almost weakened her resolve. But no, that sounded possessive and through her own choosing, she did not yet have the right to possess him. 'Never mind. Is it a conference?'

'Something like that. I can't get out of it, I'm afraid, or I would. And better to get it out of the way now than having it interfere with possible wedding plans.'

'Now, Frank, you're hurrying me again.' She smiled up at him.

'Do you blame me? I've had enough of delay.' He put his arms round her shoulders and pulled her gently towards him. She imagined that she could feel his heart beating inside the thin chest. Perhaps she could feel it. Perhaps he could feel hers too, two hearts beating in time. She was aware, sharply, of his vulnerability and she wanted to care for him as he cared for her.

She looked downwards, into the water. 'Look at our reflections, joined together. That's how it will be for us, Frank.' A dead leaf fell and their smiles dissolved in ripples, spreading across the surface until their happiness was disseminated and magnified a hundred times.

'That's so like you.' His lips brushed her ear. 'A lovely thought. I need you to bring gentle, joyful ideas into my life.' He kissed her and she drank in the experience, with the warm stones beneath her feet and the hot sun on her closed eyelids and the rough friendly tweed of his jacket beneath her hands. She knew at that moment that she was more alive than she had ever been before. And she was almost ready to give him the answer he wanted. But not quite.

* * *

On the day of the trip, Jen's first thought on waking was that she wished she had never agreed to do this. Her newfound optimism had vanished on reporting back to Maria and being met with Maria's easy smile. 'Thanks. I'll bear your opinion in mind. But I'd still prefer to weigh the situation up for myself.'

She had been naïve, Jen realised, to have expected anything else. And now Maria was to be set loose at Sellybrook to wreak whatever havoc she chose.

Alan was muttering and grumbling in his sleep. She wondered, not for the first time, whether she should tell him about Maria's hidden agenda. Would that make it worse? Perhaps she should just hope for the best. She was still touched that Alan had decided to come too and support her. She didn't want to cause him unnecessary pain. And what harm could Maria do when there was obviously nothing for her to find? She would just be making a fool of herself. Leave it. Be aware and be ready to step in and smooth things over if necessary. That would be best.

It was early but she was well awake now. She went downstairs, found a plastic carrier, rinsed three apples and took a handful of wrapped biscuits from the tin. She looked up as the kitchen door opened. 'Oh, hello, Alan. You didn't need to get up yet. I'm just starting on the sandwiches.'

'I had a terrible dream.' He was shaking his head, puffing out his cheeks.

'I know, love. You woke me up.'

He smiled. 'You should have thumped me. Or perhaps not. I'd gone back to when my father made Graham and I kill our rabbit. We called him Bobtail. He got caught in a snare but he was still alive when we found him. Dad said we had to kill him straightaway. Ourselves.'

Her hands stilled, clutching the tea towel. 'And this was in the dream? It wasn't what happened, surely?'

'Yes. It happened. And in the dream as well. I was suddenly back there, going to find the hammer with tears running down my face. It was horrible.'

'But couldn't you have taken him to the vet?'

'Dad said it would be cruel. Taking him all that way when he was in pain. He was too far gone. Phew, I'd forgotten all about that incident. I suppose you can block things out for years. I don't know what put that back in my head.'

'The thought of going back to the house?' Jen said in a low voice.

'Must have been. I wish I hadn't remembered it. I can't forget it again now. There was so much blood, from the snare I think, not the hammer. And then Bobtail was floating somehow, in the pool. But I think that was in the dream.'

She rested her head on his shoulder. 'It must have been awful for you. And dreams always seem worse when you first get up.'

'He said we shouldn't allow unnecessary suffering. I suppose he was right.'

A horrible thing to do to the two boys. Could the man not have dealt with the situation himself? She wished they had more time to talk about this. It would have to wait until tonight, she thought. Because now they had to get on.

She began to think Erica would never be ready. 'Come on, Mother, that handbag's fine. I want to get to the community centre before the coach arrives. To make sure people are happy with their seats. Some of them have special requirements.' Insisting on being at the back, the middle, away from the wheels. But, admit it, she wanted to be there before Maria.

'Or should I borrow that little backpack of yours after all? My goodness, that jacket's bright, Jen.'

'You don't need a backpack. And I'm wearing this orange fleece so that I'll stand out and people can find me easily if they need me.'

Alan grinned, shaking his head as he zipped his cagoule. 'Just leave them to it. Let them sort themselves out. You're trying to do too much. They won't mind.'

No, but she had to go one better than Maria. Showing off her organising skills. Childish no doubt she couldn't help how she felt. 'It's OK. Be prepared.'

'No,' Erica cried. 'My handbag will be better. I was forgetting. It's a better match with my walking shoes because the woods may be muddy.'

'Woods?' Alan swung round. 'I thought we were visiting the house.'

Jen squeezed his arm, relieved that Erica was ready at last. 'I knew you weren't listening. We shall be walking across to the Hall after lunch, through the woods. Weather permitting, that is. If it rains, we can use the coach and go down the drive. But the forecast isn't too bad. Now, Mother, can we go?'

And of course, Maria was there before them. Like the third little pig, Jen thought. Except that she was elegant in her usual black and looked nothing like a pig. Jen at once felt that she had put on too many layers and that the orange fleece had been a mistake. She had wondered in the shop whether it made her skin look sallow and thought it wouldn't matter. It had been the brightest they had. Perhaps she could leave it in the coach with all the sandwiches because her jumper was thick and she had a cagoule in her bag she could wear instead. But no, she was wearing the fleece for a good reason and why should she let Maria influence her decision?

'Hello all of you. I've been looking forward to this.' Maria's smile widened and she glanced at Alan. 'I thought the first here might as well get on already, rather than hang about. Most of them seem to be early birds. That OK?'

Jen smiled back. 'That's fine.'

'Are we waiting for anyone else?'

'Wait a minute.' Jen was counting down the list. This wasn't right, surely? How many seats were there on this coach? Somehow, between Maria's initial organisation and Jen's taking over, the numbers didn't add up. And sure enough, latecomers were milling about in the aisle, craning their necks as they searched for spaces.

Frowning concern from Maria. 'You did get that additional list I popped through your letterbox?'

Jen didn't even bother to answer her. Why was Maria doing this — ah, yes, because she was hoping to be left behind with Alan? Well, if this was a fight over Alan, there could only be one winner and it wouldn't be Maria. 'OK, there are too many people for this size of coach. We're victims of our own success. Who doesn't have a seat? Four of you. If you take our car, Alan, that will sort everything out.'

'Will do.'

Maria stood up. 'Have my seat, Nelly, and rest your legs. I don't mind going in the car.'

Nelly, handbag arrayed over one arm, gained Jen's attention with a sharp finger. 'No, thank you. I don't want Maria's seat. I never sit at the front.

Not right behind the driver.'

'That's fine, Nelly. You don't have to. You're going in our car with Alan.' She smoothly sorted it all out until they were ready to leave. She avoided looking at Maria but was grimly conscious of her victory. So far, so good. Even the driver was smirking but that might have been the gum he was chewing. Now he met Jen's eyes in the driving mirror as she sat down. He turned round. 'Is it you who's in charge, then and not the other lady? I can't be late back. I've got an evening booking.'

'No later than arranged. Back here no later than six thirty. That's right, isn't it, Maria?' They had better make that clear. But it seemed this at least was not a matter for argument. After this shaky start, the journey passed smoothly enough, although Jen was on edge, wondering what Maria might try next. But she was chatting amiably, saying nothing out of turn. And at last they were there.

Graham was standing at the edge of the shadows by the porch, as if he had never moved during the three weeks since Jen's first visit. Alan was getting out of the car, opening the doors for his passengers. He was worried about this meeting, Jen could tell. He was pulling at his sleeves and hitching into his collar.

Graham said, 'Bang on time, Jen. Well done.' He was smiling at her but his eyes were focussed on a point past her shoulder.

She turned and he was looking at Alan who was right behind her, one hand extended. 'Good to see you, Graham.' It was the impersonal voice he used for business deals.

Graham accepted the handshake and gripped Alan's elbow with his free hand, a double clasp. For a moment Alan's face seemed strained before he smiled back and they stood, hands joined, for slightly longer than necessary. Jen took a relieved breath. It was going to be all right. Alan said, 'Any

169

chance of putting my car in the garage, Graham? I don't want to get sap and leaves on the paintwork if it rains again.'

'That's fine. Plenty of room.'

Jen chuckled. Only another male would take this OTT request as perfectly reasonable. She hadn't realised just how much this meeting had worried her too. She waved one orange arm. 'OK, everyone. I think we should look at the outside of the house while the weather's still fine. If that's all right with you, Graham?' She wondered when Maria would try to slip away; discreetly, she hoped.

They were comparing mason's marks at the eastern end of the house when heavy rain bit into their faces and Jen ushered them all inside. There were exclamations of pleasure at the hall, with the stone flags and central staircase and the low wooden doors leading off. They moved through the ground floor rooms to the left, examining door lintels and wooden pegs in beams and the original flagged floor.

It was all going well. They trooped back across the hall to enter the white-painted parlour. Alan was slightly ahead of Jen; he slipped and stumbled, clutching the doorframe. Maria, already through the doorway, reached him first, taking his arm. 'Are you all right, Alan? What's the matter?'

He wasn't looking at Maria. His head was turned to look at the wall over the mantelpiece. 'Nothing. Thanks. I tripped. This floor.'

Maria said, 'Oh, I see.' Looking from Alan to the portrait of the tragic Celia Laurence.

'Do you want to sit down?' Jen suggested. Was it stress? He'd been working so hard lately, since the move.

'No, no.' He was brushing her hands away. 'I'm fine. Don't fuss. Graham, where did that painting come from?'

Graham's reply was the same as before. 'The original turned up in the attics at the hall but was in a bad condition. Simon let me borrow it to copy. It has a certain atmosphere, doesn't it?'

The exchange seemed ordinary enough but as Alan and Graham stared at each other, Jen felt that something was passing between them. Graham said, 'As you can see, an extra window has been inserted here in the nineteen sixties, giving a view of the garden at the side of the house.'

Jen opened and closed her mouth. Had he forgotten to tell the group about Celia Laurence? But it was such a good story. She hesitated, wishing she knew what had been going on between the brothers a few moments before. Yes, Graham was beginning to usher them out of the room and without even asking for questions.

Erica was at the forefront of the group however and seized her opportunity. 'And who is the lady in the portrait? One of your ancestors?'

Jen was certain she heard Maria gasp, difficult to tell from the back. But she could see the hand creeping onto Alan's shoulder. Graham was smiling at Erica. 'An unknown lady, I'm afraid.'

Jen frowned. 'But surely — ' Erica began.

'She is displaying her pain, craving an end of it, craving peace. Who can see this painting and not wish to help her somehow? But maybe she found her own solution.' His voice was matter-of-fact. Without changing his tone, he said, 'I think we had better move on upstairs or you will be having a very late lunch. I'm under orders to press on, you know, and not to get sidetracked too much. And there's an interesting chimney breast there and another walk-in cupboard. Ideal for the incarceration of disobedient children. And the blocked-up windows of course.'

'Window tax,' Harold said.

They trooped upstairs where the floorboards creaked and wobbled. Erica tried the bathroom door. 'Locked, I'm afraid,' Graham called. 'You can use the one downstairs if you like — or there's an en-suite off the main bedroom. I needed to deposit my breakables and valuables somewhere safe. Just as a precaution.'

Jen caught the look of frustration on Maria's face and smiled. If everything of importance had been locked away, that might restrain Maria a bit. Belatedly, she covered her smile with her hand.

Graham was saying, 'And now Jen is making the secret signs to me which would seem to indicate the eating of sandwiches. So if you could come downstairs again, she will talk you through the arrangements. And I've made my own packed lunch so I can join in with you all.'

Jen explained they were to eat their sandwiches in the old barn across the courtyard. 'Graham has kindly laid on tea and coffee making facilities in there.' Most of the group began crossing the drive to the coach, to collect bags and flasks.

Maria was waving, her mouth twisted with concern. 'I'm so sorry, I didn't realise we had to bring sandwiches. I thought we'd be going to a pub, as we usually do.'

'It's all right,' Alan said quickly. Too quickly? 'You can share mine.' And that seemed to result in his sharing the plastic patio table Maria chose too, in a dim and secluded corner. Jen sat next to Graham with her back towards the other two but by the time she had stood up repeatedly to make sure everyone had a drink and Graham had helped with the temperamental kettle, Alan was beside her again, screwing his sandwich bag into a ball. 'I'm going for a bit of a stroll. Won't be long.'

'Maria needs some fresh air, does she?' At once Jen wished she hadn't said that but this whole thing was getting to her now. Or Maria was. Was this part of her plan for slipping away — or something else? 'Alan, wait.' She had to call twice before he stopped. She hurried after him, out of the barn, lowering her voice. 'What about Graham? You've hardly spoken to him.

He'll think you're avoiding him.' Across the courtyard, she could see Maria waiting.

He gave her his old relaxed smile. 'No, he won't. Don't worry.'

Jen shook her head. 'Look at me, Alan.' She stared into his face, forcing him to make eye contact. 'Can't you see what Maria's trying to do?'

'She's not doing anything. She only wants to be outside.'

'Alan, you're hopeless. Maybe you're closing your eyes to it on purpose.' She had meant, so strongly, to keep these feelings to herself. But now the words came out on their own. 'She wants you back.'

'No, no.' He shook his head forcefully. 'You couldn't be more wrong. There's something she wants to tell me. It's important.'

'Oh, I see.' It was part of Maria's plan, after all. Obviously wanting to question Alan about his brother. 'Well, OK then. I'm sorry.' She hesitated. 'Sometimes I think I love you too much.'

'Impossible. You carry on with your lunch. I won't be long.'

It was nothing, Jen thought, trying to convince herself. Or not what you thought. Her lips were dry and she licked them, several times. And she wasn't reassured about Graham's feelings. He was sitting on his own now. 'I'm so sorry Alan's had to rush off. I was hoping you and he could get together more today.'

'You're a kind woman, Jen. Sensitive. But don't worry about me.' He spoke quietly. 'Alan has always been skilled in avoidance. And I knew he would find this meeting difficult — and not just because of Lisa and the affair he had with her.'

Jen stared at him. A gust of wind filled the barn with the smell of dust and dry leaves. 'You knew? Oh, I'm so sorry.'

He shrugged. 'All that was a long time ago. Our marriage had long been an empty performance and I know the affair was brief.'

Jen exhaled a long slow breath. 'It's good of you to be so forgiving. If only Alan knew, I'm sure he would have made contact more often.'

Graham sat back, crumpling the sandwich wrappings round and round in his hands. 'There's more to it, I'm afraid. He was pretty cut up when Mum died, you know and Lisa's suicide took Alan right back.'

Jen looked down at the table. 'I don't know much about it. He doesn't feel ready to talk about your mother's death. Not in any detail.'

He gave her an understanding smile. 'And Alan is always so busy filling every minute with new ideas and activities that you hardly hear what he isn't saying.'

'That's it, exactly.' She smiled back. 'I'm so glad we came here to meet you properly, Graham. Perhaps you can help me to understand Alan's feelings. He seems to be hiding so much. Everyone says how cheerful he is but submerging his emotions can't be healthy, psychologically.'

'You're right. I've come to terms with Mum's death, fifteen years ago, in my own way. Alan still needs to go through the healing process. I'll be glad to help. In fact, I may be able to instigate that process today.' The tightly crumpled papers in his hands were now hardly visible. He smiled. 'Leave it with me.'

9

Frank phoned Dorothy from France, within three days, telling her how much he missed her and could they discuss the arrangements?

'Now, Frank, you know we agreed to wait a little.' She paused. That emotional afternoon by the pool seemed distant now, a time when she had been swept away like a heroine in a full Technicolor movie. 'I'm not sure. Perhaps we should wait until both the boys have finished school.'

'Dorothy, how many years is that? One year is too long.' He coughed.

She was concerned at once. 'Are you all right?'

'Yes, fine. It's the warm sea breezes. So invigorating and doing my chest the world of good. You'd love it on this coast.' He paused. 'We could even sell both the Hall and Sellybrook and move out here permanently.'

Her head jerked with shock but he was joking, of course. 'Frank! I was taking you seriously for a moment. But you know how I feel about this house.'

'I know. It was only a thought. Something my doctor said.'

'What do you mean, Frank? What did your doctor say?'

He raised his voice. 'It's a bad line. I'll try and phone again soon. I love you, Dorothy.'

'I love you too, Frank. Goodbye, Frank, dear.' He won't be long, she thought. I'll be seeing him again soon.

Sooner than she had expected.

Dorothy had never visited the Infirmary before but there was the familiar prickling of the skin on her arms as she walked through the glass doors. All hospitals were horribly the same. None of this made sense and she didn't know why she had come. A silly rumour in the village shop and even when she had phoned the hospital and they seemed to agree that yes, Frank Parkestone was there, she still thought there must have been some mistake. He had phoned her, hadn't he? From France.

Suddenly she was round a corner and joining the queue for Ward Five where a face she knew was looking back at her. Simon Parkestone, holding a large chocolate box. She half-smiled, not knowing how to react and he looked away. She should have realised that he might be here.

'Excuse me.' A young woman, wearing a green waxed jacket, was standing in front of her. She had a pale, nondescript face and mouse-brown hair. 'Could I have a word? I'm Samantha Parkestone. I'm here with my brother.'

'Oh, I see. Dorothy Littlewood.'

'Yes, I know. I'm sorry, Mrs Littlewood but you've had a wasted journey. You won't be able to see my father.' She was looking at the wall behind Dorothy's head. 'He didn't want you to know he was here.'

Dorothy knew she would remember

every tiny detail of Samantha's face. Everything was too clear, as if she was looking through someone else's glasses. 'But you see, your father and I are very close. Couldn't you tell him I'm here?'

'It would upset him. And you don't want that, I'm sure. You'll have to excuse me, he'll be wondering where I am.' Samantha was moving away.

Grief and anger boiled up in Dorothy's chest. 'No, I'm sorry. I must see him.' She pushed Samantha aside and strode through the doors. Now she was almost running down the ward. And he was there, his face pale and thin above the grey striped pyjamas. She had never seen him without a tie before. He looked lost and vulnerable. But he smiled and coughed as she ran to him. 'Dorothy. I knew you'd come.'

She was biting back a sob, trying to speak calmly. 'I had to see you, Frank, I'm sorry.' She glanced round but there was no sign of Samantha — and Simon was already retreating. 'Your daughter said I hadn't to come.'

He shifted against the pillow, wincing as he bent his elbows. 'It's difficult, you see. The medical staff are making a big fuss about nothing. Until I get the results of my tests and we know what's wrong — ' He grasped her hand. 'They say its all for the best but I think their opinions are exaggerated nonsense.'

'But what is wrong? I mean, what are the symptoms?' She grasped one hand as he nodded, tapping his chest. 'Your heart? Oh, I see. You should have told me. I had no idea.'

He shook his head. 'They're very strict in here. Now if we could tell them that you are my fiancée, you would have every right to see me. Even Matron couldn't argue with that.'

'Oh, Frank.' She was laughing and crying at the same time. 'Trust you to make use of a horrible situation in order to get what you want.'

'If it brings me the wife I long for, Dorothy, I shan't regret all this unpleasantness. Will you think again? Please? I have to admit this little fiasco has frightened me. I have never felt my age so keenly. Will you marry me, Dorothy? As soon as I get out of here?'

How could she have been so stupid? All her objections were nothing but excuses. 'I will. Of course I will. I don't know why I've delayed so much. All I want is to be with you.' For as long as we have left. She pushed the thought away.

He kissed her cheek. 'You've made me so happy.'

'I'll come and see you again tomorrow.'

He frowned. 'They're starting the tests tomorrow. I don't want you to be trailing in needlessly. I'll phone you.'

She drove home on a sea of bubbles and the elation stayed with her through giving the boys the glad tidings and drinking a solemn toast in Vimto. But the next morning, anxiety began to edge into the joy. Surely Frank should have found something out by now?

She got the vacuum cleaner out, without thinking. Halfway across the rug, she remembered she had to listen for the phone and switched it off. She might have missed it already but no, she was sure she hadn't. Frank must be having problems getting hold of the telephone trolley.

She sat down with a cup of coffee and a chocolate digestive. When the phone did ring at last, she jumped and the biscuit snapped in her hand. There, you see, Frank had kept his word. She licked chocolate from her fingers as she picked the phone up.

'Mrs Littlewood?' Samantha's voice was the same, smooth and cool. 'I'm sorry to have to tell you that my father died last night.'

Time stopped and froze. 'I beg your pardon?'

Samantha was continuing as if reading from a prepared statement. 'At three a.m., peacefully. It was sudden at the end but not unexpected.'

Not unexpected by who? Samantha herself, the nursing staff? 'Died? I don't know what you mean.'

'A heart attack. You knew about his weak heart? Now, do you want me to let you know about the arrangements?'

He couldn't be dead. Not Frank. It was only hours since she had spoken to him, holding his warm, dry hand. If only she had known sooner. There was so much she could have said. Should have said.

She looked round the room, surprised that everything still looked the same. Except that somehow the two halves of biscuit were on the floor by her chair. She picked them up and tried to fit them together. But they wouldn't fit. Too many crumbs were missing. She ate a piece from each half, slowly, like Alice in Wonderland in the hall with the pool of tears. This way, the two halves would intermingle as she ate them. It was the only way it could be done.

And the halves would be changed forever too. They would no longer be chocolate digestive. But that didn't matter. Life is change, she thought. You have to remember that. That's how it is. She sank down onto the floor abruptly, as if someone had chopped at the backs of her knees.

She must have sat there unmoving for over an hour while her brain tried to make sense of this disordered day. What was she thinking of? Soon she must be ready for the boys coming home. Yes, her boys. She needed them and at once. She only needed her boys and she would get through this, she would.

A key in the lock. Alan using his own key to let them in. They would wonder why she had not been keeping watch on her hill. She held out her arms to them. They were helping her up, gently. 'Sit down, Mum,' Alan said. 'Whatever's happened?'

She sat, shaking her head, unable to say anything.

Graham knelt beside her chair. 'It's Frank, isn't it?'

From now on, she would leave everything to the boys. They would look after her.

188

* * *

'Jen,' Graham said, 'this is Simon Parkestone. He's going to escort us over to the Hall.'

Jen nodded. 'It's good of you to go to so much trouble.'

Simon shrugged, without smiling. 'I didn't want anyone straying from the path and disturbing the game.' Tall and spare, wearing a well-worn waxed jacket and carrying a walking stick.

The brusque greeting didn't seem to worry Graham. 'And you remember my brother, Alan?'

'Yes, I do.' Simon's mouth twitched at one side. Almost a smile. 'You were going to get back to me about that piece of land. Years ago.'

'Land? Ah, so I was. Sorry about that.' Alan shook his head. 'I never dismissed the idea.'

'When Graham moved back here, I thought it would be the perfect opportunity to reinstate negotiations. But he tells me he can't make a move without your say-so and we never see you. I didn't think you would be the sort to bear a grudge, Alan.'

Neither the time nor the place to be plumbing such depths, Jen thought, whatever he was talking about. She said cheerfully, 'Oh, Alan, I know you've got a terrible memory but how on earth could you forget something like that? And for so long?' Around them, the group were watching and listening with interest. 'Shall we set off?' Nobody moved.

'You know me,' Alan said. 'It was never intentional, Simon. And we may well be able to do something about it now. We're not in a position to buy the land ourselves but we shall be putting this house on the market shortly. So we could tell prospective purchasers that the land is available. Couldn't we, Graham?'

Somebody coughed. Feet shuffled on the gravel. Jen was aware of the breeze chilling her cheeks. She opened her mouth and couldn't speak. Graham had taken refuge in stillness as if his mind had withdrawn behind the empty facade of his face.

'Good,' Simon said. 'I'll get back to you on that. I'll take a contact number before you leave. Had we better be moving?'

Graham allowed the others to swirl past him before coming to life. 'How long have you been planning this, Alan?'

'Selling the house?' Alan scratched his ear. 'Not long. But it's hardly a surprise, is it, Graham?' There was a pleading note in his voice. 'We all knew this could only be a temporary bolt-hole for you. You said that yourself. And you'll get half the proceeds.'

'That's not the point.' Graham was speaking without inflection. He pushed past the others on the path, to join Simon at the front.

Jen said, 'That wasn't the best way of doing it, Alan.' And she was as bad. She should have said something to Graham herself, three weeks ago. Tried to prepare him.

191

'No, perhaps not.' He was lowering his head and hunching his shoulders, like a guilty teenager. 'There's been so much that's happened, here. More than you know.'

Maria had broken away from the retreating group to come back for them. 'Come on, you two. You'll be left behind.' She was taking Alan's arm.

Something inside Jen snapped. 'You carry on, Alan. Wait a minute, Maria. I'd like a word. It won't take long.' She waited a moment until Alan's long legs had carried him out of hearing. 'I want to know what's going on. You could have spoken to Alan any time. What did you have to say that was supposedly so important? Or was that just an excuse to get him on his own?'

Maria was half-smiling. 'I don't know what you mean.'

'Yes, you do. You're making it so obvious. He's my husband but you'd have him back like a shot.'

Maria stared at her, the sun catching the green flecks in her eyes. 'I thought you understood. We were talking about Alan's relationship with Lisa. You must see that the affair gives him a motive. I have to be quite certain in my own mind that Alan can be eliminated.'

Furious phrases tumbled in Jen's head. How dare she? Maria was lying obviously. Trying to push Jen into anger. Anger meant loss of control and a small victory for Maria. This was merely part of the game. Maria was testing Jen's love and loyalty. To win, Jen had to stay calm, because the woman was completely deluded. She took a deep breath. 'Of course you do. I'm glad we've been able to get that straight. As you said, we're a team and must work together.' She nodded and smiled.

Maria, she could tell, wasn't sure whether to believe in this reaction or not. She looked closely into Jen's face, said, 'OK then,' and set off along the path to join the group next to Alan. Taking his arm. He smiled down at her.

Jen forced her steps to remain unhurried. Where the path widened a little, Erica was waiting for her. Oh, no, Jen thought. All I need. 'Bold as brass,' Erica muttered. 'He's getting entangled with that little madam and you're shutting your eyes to it.'

'No, I'm not. But I'm not going to provide an entertainment for the local history group by doing something about it now. Bad enough that they've witnessed the problem with the house.'

'You must stand up for yourself.'

'I will, believe me. Oh, yes. But not now.'

They left the main path and turned onto a narrow track through the brambles and nettles. Without warning, they were out into a natural clearing. Jen had a confusing sight of the group in double vision before realising they were standing around a pool of water, filled with light beyond the upside-down figures, reflecting the bright sky and hurried clouds. The magic of the place dispelled Jen's anger. She called, 'You never told me about this, Alan.'

He was standing behind her, two

steps back and where the trees began again. Somewhere along the path he had picked up a fallen branch he was leaning on as if it was a walking stick. All around the pool, the others were smiling, murmuring compliments, phones and cameras held upwards. She raised her own camera.

'Be careful,' Graham was saying. 'The stones can be slippery.'

'Is it deep?' someone asked.

'Deep enough. We used to swim here as boys, didn't we, Alan?' There was no sign of his previous bitterness. 'Do you remember that summer, Alan, and how happy we were? And those naval battles with the boats we made with twigs and paper?'

'And who won?' Maria cried.

'No one. It was never fully resolved, was it?' He didn't wait for an answer. 'Many of the legends that go with the house seem to be centred round this pool. There have been several drownings here: accidental, suicide and even murder.'

His audience rippled. Somewhere behind Jen, she felt an angry, brushing movement. Turning, she saw Alan was stabbing the undergrowth with the branch. Graham waited a moment or two, milking the tension. 'Celia Laurence drowned herself here when she was jilted.' No one could accuse him of avoiding the legends now; he was adding all the necessary blood-curdling details to bring happy squeaks from his listeners.

Harold interrupted, using his chairman's voice. 'These minor incidents tend to attract graphic and often spurious detail in the retelling. Has anyone ever noted a sacrificial element here, Graham? I feel that the legends contain all the elements of the typical Celtic triple death ceremonies. They could provide an interesting throwback to when the chosen sacrificial victim was clubbed, strangled and drowned as an offering to the gods. Perhaps the result of communal memory.'

Graham's face seemed flushed. 'Certainly. Local historians agree with that.'

Jen squealed as Alan pushed past her and her feet slid on the moss. Erica caught her by the arm. 'Good heavens, Alan. Jen was nearly in the pool.'

'No, it's OK. I'm fine.' Jen was watching Alan as he thrust his way through the others to face his brother.

'What the hell are you playing at? Let's stick to facts and move on to the Hall, shall we?' They stood for a moment, confronting each other, their eyes on a level. Jen stared at them, holding her breath. What was happening? This wasn't the Alan she knew. He rarely displayed anger. If he happened to be annoyed about something, he would take a long walk and forget about it, returning his usual cheerful self and full of something else.

Simon said, 'Any time. Whenever you're ready.' The moment had passed. Heads had turned but it was unlikely that anyone knew what was going on, Jen thought. She didn't know herself. Had Graham upset Alan deliberately in return for the unwelcome news about the sale of the house? But she didn't know what he had said to trigger Alan's reaction.

People began to pick their way round the pool and back to the main path. Alan threw the stubby branch down onto the stones and pushed his hands deep into his pockets again. Jen could see the waterproof material straining at the shoulders. She wanted to go to him but didn't know what to say and while she hesitated, Maria was there before her. She looked to be squeezing his arm in silent sympathy.

As they set off along the path, led by Simon, Maria was pausing again. 'How far did you say it was?' She rubbed her thin sleeves with both hands. 'I think I should run back to the coach for my coat. No, it's all right, Alan. You go on ahead. I'll soon catch up.'

'No, I'll come with you. The path isn't always clear and I know the way.' Like a puppet, Jen thought. Making exactly the response Maria wanted. But you could hardly blame Alan. He was obviously still upset and wouldn't be thinking straight.

Jen slipped past her mother. 'Maria? No need for you to be left behind. I have a cagoule in my bag. You can have that.'

'Oh. Thanks.' Maria managed a grateful smile. 'But I don't think that will be thick enough. I chose to wear a thin shirt because my coat had such a warm lining.'

And more fool you, if that was true. But Jen knew this was not about linings and sleeves. 'You can have this fleece — and I'll wear the cagoule. If we walk briskly, you'll soon warm up.' She smiled at Maria as if she hadn't a care in the world. Keep her guessing. Maria seemed to have run out of arguments. Her thanks as she put on Jen's fleece were over the top. Jen said cheerfully, 'No problem. Anytime.' And Alan, she was pleased to see, was striding ahead without waiting for either of them.

As a house, Martonby Hall was disappointing. Sellybrook was by far the more homely and atmospheric of the two. The Hall was shabbily Georgian and had a cold, unlit feel even after their invigorating walk with the clouds massing overhead and the wind strengthening. By now, however, Jen hardly cared whether her charges were impressed or not.

'Nice to be shown around a house that feels so lived in,' Grace Smithson said, kindly. The communal nods were too enthusiastic to be convincing. But Simon Parkestone didn't seem the sort who would be worried by the opinions of others. It was surprising and fortunate that he had agreed to this at all, from what Graham had said.

Erica pulled at her arm. 'He must be struggling financially,' she whispered. Yes, best not to look too closely at the sparse and faded furnishings and empty spaces where paintings had been. Jen found all this embarrassing; it was obvious he did need the money he would get from selling the piece of woodland.

'Well, thank you, Simon, that was fascinating.' Jen rushed into her prepared speech as they returned to the entrance hall. 'Seeing round your house has been an unexpected privilege. And most interesting to discover how Martonby Hall and Sellybrook mesh together historically.'

Simon nodded. 'Yes. I'll see you to the boundary.'

Jen shook her head. 'There's no need. Really. We've taken up enough of your time as it is.' He was ignoring her protests and taking his walking stick from the cast iron umbrella stand. She said, 'Well, if you'd rather.'

Out on the drive, she moved over to Alan. 'What a strange man,' she muttered. 'Was he always like this?'

'What? Oh, yes. Pretty much. We didn't have much to do with him. He was a few years older than we were. There was just one summer — well, never mind.'

Jen was watching the thin lithe energy striding away. 'He can't be so much older than you, surely? But I suppose a gap of a few years makes a big difference when you're a child.'

'And when our mother happened to be falling in love with his father. That made things a bit tense between Simon and us.'

'What? I didn't know about that.'

'No, it doesn't matter.' He was looking down at the ground as he walked. 'Some other time.'

'I'm sorry if coming back here stirred things up for you.' Once again he was acting like a different person. Her Alan, the one she had always known, would have squeezed her shoulders and told her not to worry. Always ready to make light of their problems.

He said, 'Hmm.' Without touching her.

She put her arm round him instead. 'You should have told me if you didn't want to come. I kept saying you didn't have to.'

He said bitterly, 'It would have made no difference if I had told you.'

202

Jen said quietly, 'Coming here was Maria's idea. You know that.'

'But you jumped at it.'

'Alan — ' She stood in front of him so he had to stop too. One or two stragglers made their way past but Jen couldn't have said who they were. She hardly saw them. 'Alan, just what is wrong?'

He made an angry chopping gesture with his arms. 'I don't know why he's doing this to me. Does he think it was my fault? I wasn't even here. I found her and they said she'd been there for hours.' He put a hand over his mouth as if trying to keep the words back. 'Our mother drowned herself in that pool. They said she was ill, officially that the balance of her mind was disturbed.'

'Oh, Alan, I'm so sorry.'

He shrugged. 'I thought I could cope with coming back here, after all this time. Shows how wrong you can be. But I wouldn't have come anywhere near if it hadn't been for this stupid outing. We should have sold it in the first place. Got rid of it. But Graham wanted to hang on.'

'I can see why you have to sell. I'm sorry. I didn't understand.'

'How could you? You never knew my mother.' He managed to make that sound like a reproach.

Jen said gently, 'I can hardly help that. I wish I could have met her.'

Alan said nothing. He jerked away from her, along the path, to end up inevitably by the landmark of the orange fleece. Everything Jen said seemed to be wrong and she didn't know why when she only wanted to help him. And briefly there, she had felt they were becoming close again. Had Maria known Alan's mother? If so she held an advantage Jen could never match.

No, she was being a fool. She and Alan had something so good together; they had both known it from the beginning. He was only turning to Maria today because he was reliving the bygone turmoil and Maria belonged to his past. And now Maria was hanging on to Alan's arm and nodding solemnly. Seizing yet another chance to show how supportive she could be when her true intention was to undermine the one family relationship he still possessed. By seeking to incriminate Graham in Lisa's death. If Maria had been telling the truth about that. Jen no longer knew what to believe.

They were almost back at Sellybrook and now Jen must make her final speech before letting them all loose on their free time. She raised her voice. 'We have just over an hour left, which you can spend as you like. The house again, the grounds or more tea and coffee in the barn. And Graham has kindly agreed to open his library for anyone interested in his collection. But whatever you do, could we have you back at the coach for five fifteen, please? No later. And can you all show your appreciation to Graham for allowing us to make use of his home? And to Simon too.' Because for some reason, he was still hanging about. The applause was sincere and Graham smiled, made a self-deprecating gesture and murmured, 'A pleasure.'

Simon nodded. There, almost done. Jen wouldn't be sorry to see the last of this outing. No doubt Harold and the society would consider it a success but it had thrown up too many complications to handle in one day. They would be home for half past six. Bliss. All she wanted was to get home and snuggle up on the sofa with Alan and a glass of wine.

But a small niggling feeling was telling her that half past six was still a long way off.

10

Dorothy could hardly remember the funeral, a blessing she supposed. But she knew it hadn't seemed real. Graham kept saying, 'Don't cry, Mum, please.' She didn't weep. It was a grief beyond tears.

Later, she wished she had been less self-absorbed. She had forgotten how Samantha and Simon must have been feeling. She should have approached them, offering what comfort she could.

When Simon Parkestone phoned, asking to make an appointment to see her, she knew she had been given another chance. Dorothy chose to wear a dark suit with a white blouse. That seemed appropriate. But Simon Parkestone was wearing his usual waxed jacket and green wellingtons. She looked at the boots doubtfully. 'Would you like to come into the parlour?'

He muttered, 'Said the spider to the fly.'

'I beg your pardon?' She must have misheard. 'Would you like sherry? Or would you prefer coffee or tea?'

'I'm not bothered, thanks. I'd rather get on with it.' He sat down before she had invited him to sit. 'The thing is, Mrs Littlewood, I've come about that piece of land Dad bought from you.'

'To make a new drive, yes.' He was sitting where Frank had so often sat and now she could see a likeness to Frank which she had never noticed before, in the way he held his head. And of course the colour of his eyes. She found that comforting, a little.

'Not exactly essential for us, was it? He never got round to building it. I don't suppose he was ever going to. We both know he only took it to help you out.'

'Perhaps so.' She smiled at the memory. That had been so like Frank.

'And now I want you to buy it back. Dad's death has left us with a lot of expense. I hope you're going to be reasonable. It's because of you and all your delaying tactics that the biggest deal, the one that would have secured our future, came to nothing.'

No, he was not like Frank at all. Dorothy straightened her back against the stiff cushions. 'It isn't a question of being reasonable. I don't have the money any more. And what do you mean about the biggest deal?'

His eyes were half closed as he ignored her question. 'No, you didn't need to be careful with money, did you? Dad was a soft touch. Falling in love at his age, like an old fool. He slipped up, badly. You can't mix love and business.'

Dorothy gulped, staring in fascination at Frank's eyes in the thin, spiteful face. 'That's a terrible thing to say. I loved your father. We loved each other. And I would help if I could.'

He grinned. 'You didn't realise how near the edge he was, did you? No, you thought he represented a nice, safe future for you. But it was the other way round. You represented financial salvation for him. He was thinking he would have to sell the French business, his pride and joy that he'd built up from scratch himself. And then out of the blue comes this incredible opportunity to sell the Hall instead. To a property developer.'

'The Hall? Surely not? He wouldn't have sold the family home.'

'He didn't give a tuppenny toss for it. Always hated it. I care more for it than he ever did. But there was one snag. The developers were only interested if your house could be part of the deal too.'

'This house?'

'Don't keep repeating everything. Of course this house. Your land bites right into ours when you look at the map. Anyway, you know all this because they approached you, asking you to sell. That's right, isn't it?'

Dorothy was finding this too difficult to unravel. She didn't even want to untangle it. 'I don't understand. There was a letter I think, yes. More than one but I threw them away. I thought they were part of Malcolm's tricks. It was Malcolm, wasn't it? That other letter I got, thanking me; I know that was odd but it was Malcolm. So I thought, the others . . . ' Her voice trailed away.

'Yes, you really do believe that, don't you? Like you thought it was Malcolm who set out to frighten you that weekend.' He shook his head and went on shaking it. 'I know that was what Dad wanted you to think. All the same, I didn't see how anyone could be that simple. But it's true.'

'It was Malcolm. It was.' She was staring at him. Staring at Frank's blue eyes in the thin face and the mouth opening and closing while the cruel words came out and wouldn't stop.

'It would be that quality of naïve innocence that Dad fell for.' He was smiling as if pleased with his deduction. 'I see that now. It would make him feel powerful. Dad liked to know where he was with people. Liked to be in control.

That was why he never liked me much. But he wasn't in control with you either, was he? He never got what he really wanted.'

Her throat was dry, like wood shavings. 'But I'd agreed to marry him as soon as he left hospital. Didn't he tell you?'

'No, no.' His hand was thumping the arm of the chair, where Frank's hand had rested so often. 'I'm talking about the house. Your house. The house that was only part yours until Dad got your ex-husband to gift you his half with a bribe of some dicey shares. A substantial number, so large that anyone would fall for it, particularly someone who knew nothing about the stock market. But Dad's little wheezes were always convincing.' He leaned forward. 'The thing about Dad was that he always got what he wanted, whatever it took. He couldn't buy the house from you, even if you'd agreed to sell, because of the old lady's covenant. So he had a long-term plan of marrying you and

212

moving to France for health reasons — very regrettable but couldn't be helped. But he ran out of time. You weren't playing. You seem so frail and delicate but you were much tougher than Malcolm.' He laughed suddenly. 'I have to say, I admired you that weekend.'

He was silent now as if waiting for her to catch up and work it out. She felt sick. A nausea that gripped from her stomach to her throat. And her brain, which had been so unwilling to function ten minutes earlier, was now making connections only too well. The dark, the breathing, the blood and dead fur, all made a horrible sense. She gripped the chair seat to stop herself swaying backwards. 'Frank? He wanted the house so much that he allowed me to go through that ordeal? The dead rabbit in the car?'

Simon looked down at his hands, half-smiling. 'It wasn't quite like that. The original idea was his. Just to make things a bit frightening for you, he thought. But he did set everything up, instructing your husband to send for the boys so you'd be on your own. And engineering a wild goose chase of a diversion so it would look as if Malcolm had had the opportunity. And then he left the details to someone else.'

She said, 'You mean he left the details to you.'

'Yes.' He shrugged and grinned as if expecting his cleverness to be applauded. 'I know I got carried away. It was like a game. And I do regret the rabbit. Dad hauled me over the coals about that.'

Dorothy shook her head. The experience seemed distant and terrifying, the stuff of Alfred Hitchcock, but she felt now as if it had happened to someone else. And all that horror had been set in train by this misguided young man, sitting in front of her almost like a mischievous small boy. Now he seemed ordinary and harmless. She felt deflated. All the fury she had directed at Malcolm was siphoned away, leaving her with a terrible sadness.

Now she was mourning Frank all over again. The man she had thought she loved had never existed. She said, quietly, 'How could you do it? I've never done anything to hurt you.'

He stared at her. 'Only by being here. And who you are.'

'I suppose so.' And there had been the scissors, the fury in the destruction of the shredded hiking socks. She had attributed that to Malcolm's warped jealousy — not wanting her himself but not wanting anyone else to have her either. But no, it had been a child's cry at losing the father he had never held in the first place.

He stood up. 'You're sure there's no chance of buying the land back? I'm selling off the French package but this would tide me over.'

She shook her head, experiencing a sliver of compassion for him in spite of what he'd done. But not knowing how to handle Frank's betrayal. That was so much worse. 'I can't. I'm sorry.'

He nodded. 'I'll see myself out.'

The cold began in her muscles and invaded her heart. As if Frank had died all over again. As he had. And worse. Because yes, the Frank she loved had never been. She had invented him. Invented an ideal that had to be as different from Malcolm as possible. But Frank hadn't been different. Underneath he had been every bit as bad as Malcolm. Worse, because Frank had set out deliberately to deceive. Like his father and grandfather and the whole corrupt lineage, deceit came as naturally as breathing.

When the boys came home from school, they knew at once that something was wrong. She had splashed her red-rimmed eyes with cold water but her face was still white and death-like. She tried to say, 'Hello, boys,' as cheerfully as possible but the words became a sob.

They sat her down and made her a cup of tea, as they often did at the first sign of weakness. She didn't want to tell them but the more she assured them that nothing was wrong, the more they insisted, until she had to go through Simon's visit word by word.

'That was a lousy thing to say.' Graham squeezed her hand and she winced; she always forgot how strong his grip had become since he'd gained the Bullworker. 'I bet it wasn't true. I bet he made the whole thing up.'

She sighed. 'Why should he?'

Alan said quickly, 'Because he hated his father.' Always so ready to leap in without thinking.

'No, I don't think he did. In spite of the socks.' Concentration was difficult. She knew her voice sounded flat. Everything was flat. She kept trying to tell herself that Frank had loved her in his own way. But that hadn't been her way. This was like loving a stranger. 'He didn't hate him altogether. No, Simon was often kind to Frank.' She cast about for an example. 'Why, the last time I saw them together in the hospital, he had taken Frank a lovely big box of chocolates. A big gold-rimmed box with a picture of a country cottage.'

'Suppose,' Alan said. 'Though it's easy enough to buy chocolates. They had one of those boxes in the village shop for ages. And perhaps you only buy a really big box when you feel guilty.'

She tried to smile. 'So if you buy me chocolates, I'll know what it means.'

'That's right. Are you OK, Gray?'

Dorothy turned to where Graham was sitting huddled on the edge of his chair. So sensitive. He had always admired Frank. She reached out a hand. 'I know this has been very upsetting for all of us. But don't worry, we'll cope.'

And somehow, they did cope.

A year passed and now Alan had taken his A-levels and was going to university, and for Dorothy, the joy of his success was tempered by regret. His departure would be like another bereavement, all over again. Silly to feel that when she would still see him frequently, but she couldn't help herself.

Autumn again — and the sun through the golden yellow leaves had never been so bright. Gleaming spiders' webs, dew catching the last of the summer sun. She would never feel the same way about September again and the bittersweet juice of ripe blackberries. And as always now, she avoided the pool with those memories of Frank and how she had been so foolishly happy there, just one autumn ago.

She and Alan were alone in the house together during the last ripe days as Graham had gone back to school. She tried so hard to be sensible. 'Graham will miss you too. You always get on so well. Not fighting like some brothers do.'

'I'll phone you both. And he'll enjoy having you all to himself, without me butting in all the time.' Alan was gently laughing at her. But he had no idea of how she felt. For him, everything was new and exciting. 'And in a year or so, he'll be off into the big world himself. You'll be going through all this A-level business and celebrating again.' He stopped at last, obviously seeing the horror in her eyes. She couldn't help it. He said, 'Sorry, Mum. I didn't think. But by the time he goes, I'll be finishing. I'll be home by then.'

And he meant it, Dorothy was sure of that. She swallowed. 'No, you'll meet a nice girl and fall in love and set off into the sunset. That's how life is. How it should be.'

He left and she had to get used to it but he often came home, just as he had said he would. And eventually he brought a girl with him, slender and vulnerable with a delicate face and large dark eyes. 'This is Maria,' Alan said, hands pushed deeply into the pockets of his jeans; no wonder his pockets were always going into holes.

Maria's smile was shy. 'Hello, Mrs Littlewood. Oh, I knew I would like you. After all, we have Alan in common, don't we?'

Dorothy held out her arms, ready to enfold Maria to her heart. 'Oh, Alan, you have done well. How clever of you.' She so wanted to like Maria; she hoped she had sounded sincere. Even thinking about sharing him was painful but she was determined not to show it.

And it was very easy to like Maria. She was ready to chatter easily and when Dorothy dared to drop a hint about the size of the house, if Alan should possibly find a job locally, Maria responded with enthusiasm. 'I see exactly what you mean. It would be so easy to convert the living accommodation. And it would be a wonderful place to live. I love it already.'

This was surely enough to give her hope for the future, Dorothy thought. Speaking to Alan alone was a little more difficult, as it always had been, and that weekend he was either with Maria or finding a hundred and one essential things to do. She managed it at last, however, when he was packing his things together again. Dorothy sat down on his bed, adjusting the tumbled blankets to make room for herself.

'Maria is such a sweet girl, Alan. She could almost be the daughter I never had.' She knew she shouldn't ask but she had to know. She leaned forwards. 'Tell me, are you serious about her? Is she to be the one?'

He was unfolding socks, arranging them one on top of the other. 'Don't rush me, Mum.'

'Oh, no, I wouldn't do that. But you must know, inside yourself. What do you feel?'

The socks dropped into his open bag in a bundle. 'Well, yes. I suppose we might make a go of it.'

He had been cagey but overall, she was pleased with the conversation. She waved them off at the station with a light heart, envisaging a warm future that included her son and his wife and a family. She would never need to give way to loneliness. 'I've so enjoyed meeting you, Maria. You're welcome here any time.'

'Thank you so much, Mrs Littlewood. I love this house.'

But Dorothy would never see Maria again.

Alan broke the news over the phone and she had to sit down, clutching onto the wrought iron of the telephone shelf with pale fingers. 'But Alan, what on earth went wrong? You were so happy together. Surely this is just a lover's tiff and you can patch things up?'

'I don't think so.'

'But surely, she seemed such a sweet girl, will she not change her mind? If I spoke to her — '

'It was me. I finished it.'

He might as well have punched her in the stomach. She could hardly breathe. 'But why?'

'Sometimes things aren't right. You have to be certain. Look at you and Dad.'

'But I watched you together. You were right for each other. I know you were. Like two halves of a biscuit.'

He said softly, 'I know you thought

so but it didn't feel right to me.'

'Yes, I see.' Grief was swelling inside her and all her other griefs were contributing to the hurt. All the unhappiness she had thought was under control. Once she gave way to it and started weeping, she wouldn't be able to stop.

And what was Alan talking about now? She had forgotten to listen. He was saying, 'Don't you think Graham should get out more? Being stuck in the old house with you. I don't think it's doing either of you any good.'

Once she had understood everything Alan had said, almost before he spoke. They had been so close. But here was something else that didn't make sense. She said listlessly, 'We're fine.'

11

Jen took her digital camera out of her pocket and walked across the drive. Some time to herself at last, while Graham was entertaining the enthusiasts in the library. The light out here was changing all the time. Subtle shadows moved across the stonework as the wind shifted the willow branches and the bark rubbed and creaked. Through the camera, Jen saw a miniature Alan coming out of the woods to her right, walking quickly with his head bent. And on his own. She smiled at that, took a shot of the house and lowered the camera. She couldn't see Alan now. Perhaps he had gone round into the courtyard. She went to have a closer look at the porch. What had Graham told them about it? Had it been added later? She took a few close-ups of the door.

There was a thrashing of bushes and undergrowth and Maria came running out of the trees. Maria with her hair close to her scalp, her clothes dark and heavy. Her black boots were squelching a trail of wet droplets. 'The pool!' Maria was almost incoherent, shaking and crying. 'Someone pushed me in the pool.'

Jen grasped Maria's shoulders. 'It's all right. It's all right. You're safe now.' She waited for the shivering to stop, while Maria took several deep breaths. 'Listen, it doesn't seem very likely. Perhaps you slipped.'

'I'm not a fool,' Maria said indignantly. 'I was pushed.'

'Did you see who it was?'

Maria wiped her face with a dripping sleeve. 'No. Someone came up behind me and shoved me in the back.'

The disturbance had gained attention. Too much to hope that it wouldn't. Alan had appeared with some of the others, looking concerned. He said, 'We must get you home. Thank goodness I have the car.'

Was this just another way of gaining attention? Jen wondered. Was this another of Maria's plans to allow her to be alone with Alan? No, too extreme surely, even for her. Jen said, 'That would take far too long. She'd catch her death. Let's see what Graham can offer.'

★ ★ ★

'Yes.' Maria was suddenly looking much better. 'I only need a good towelling and my coat is on the coach. I can wear that.'

Jen pushed the front door open and Graham was standing in the hall. She smiled. Some people had the convenient knack of always being in the right place at the right time. Thankfully, he understood the situation at once. No pointless questions or needless explanations. 'Don't worry. We'll soon sort you out. Follow me, girls.'

Graham led Jen and Maria upstairs

and showed them into a large bedroom overlooking the drive, which had not formed part of his tour. 'This was my mother's room.' He opened the large oak wardrobe. 'Help yourselves. I'm only glad they can be of use to someone. They had been up in the loft for years until I came back here. There's an en-suite shower room, see, and plenty of hot water.' He reached out for the fleece as Maria struggled out of it and stepped across the room, wringing it out over the washbasin as he spoke, with strong, efficient movements. 'The main bathroom is locked as I told you before. OK, I'll leave you to it. You mustn't stand about. I'll take this and finish it off and there's a polythene bag in the bottom of the wardrobe for the rest of your wet clothes.'

'Thanks. We're really grateful,' Jen said.

'Yes, this is so kind of you.' Maria seemed much too cheerful considering the ordeal she had just undergone.

There was no sign of her previous histrionics.

The door closed behind Graham. Suddenly Jen understood. She turned on Maria angrily. 'Couldn't you find a less dramatic excuse for being left up here on your own?'

'I was pushed, Jen — and where was Alan when it happened? I'd only been talking to him five minutes before. I know you don't believe me but there's no time for that now. Find me something to wear and then you can make a start on going through these drawers.'

'You heard what Graham said. Everything of value is locked in the bathroom. There's nothing of importance in here.' But Maria had wasted no time and Jen's voice was lost in the noise of the shower. She was left alone with the contents of Dorothy's wardrobe. Her hands were shaking as she reached out to touch the clothes hangers. Dorothy had been a beige, cream and brown person and slim too.

Jen found a pair of sepia polyester slacks and added a couple of jumpers and a dark trouser suit that had hardly dated at all. She hated doing this. It was too intimate and how would Alan feel if he could see her, handling these long-forgotten garments?

Graham, however, hadn't seemed to mind. He was able to talk about his mother in a balanced and sensible way. But sadly Alan had to block it all out, burying his head in the sand as usual. More and more, as the day wore on, she was realising just how much Alan needed her help. And she loved him and would provide the help he needed but she was beginning to wonder whether she might be out of her depth. What if Maria was telling the truth? What if Alan had pushed her?

She didn't want to let her thoughts take that direction. Searching the room seemed preferable. She tried a couple of drawers which were empty. There was a key in a jar on the dressing table.

Nothing in this room seemed to be locked. Could this be the key to the bathroom? Although why leave it in such an obvious place?

Perhaps she should try it at least. Maria would be itching to try and would no doubt be a great deal less discreet than Jen would be. She slipped out onto the landing. Holding her breath, she pushed the key into the lock; it turned easily. Somewhere below her, another door banged. Jen, startled, locked the bathroom door again and shrank back against the wall.

There were voices in the hall. Alan said, 'You're playing games, aren't you? I don't think I ever understood you.' She recognised Graham's voice but didn't catch his reply.

Jen shot back into the bedroom, breathing quickly. Maria had finished in the shower and was thrusting herself into the trouser suit and a jumper. 'What have you found?' She nodded as Jen explained. 'Right. I'll go in and give the bathroom a quick once over when they've gone and you can stand guard in the hall.'

Jen's fingers tightened around the key. 'Maria, I really don't think this is fair on Graham. Particularly when he's been so helpful today. Lisa committed suicide. End of. I've seen nothing to make me think otherwise and the sooner you accept that the better.'

Maria hunched her shoulders in frustration. 'How can I? If it wasn't Graham, it had to be Alan.'

The blood was leaving Jen's face. 'What? You can't mean that.'

'Alan had the opportunity — and the motive, if their affair became an embarrassment to him. You may feel secure with Alan but you haven't known him long. There's so much you can't possibly know. You didn't even know, did you, that the portrait of Celia Laurence looks very like Dorothy, Alan's mother? That was why he was so upset when he first saw it. I'm sorry, Jen.' She stepped forwards, raising a hand as if to stroke Jen's shoulder to console her.

Jen twitched away. 'Don't you dare feel sorry for me.'

'Well, we'll see. If you don't want to be the lookout and check on Graham for me, it doesn't matter. I quite understand.'

Jen glared at her. The trouser suit fitted Maria perfectly and her skin was glowing from the shower. Beyond Maria, she could see herself reflected in the wardrobe mirror. Pale, harassed and homely, as her mother would have said. She turned quickly and went down the stairs, not trusting herself to speak.

Leave it for now. Best to leave Maria to get on with it. Finding nothing would shut her up. Forget Maria. Jen was sick of all this.

She went into the library. Jack and his wife, two of the most studious, were still there, huddled over a pile of books and hardly seeming to notice her. Yes, she could sit here quietly for a few minutes and allow the peace to wash over her. She rested her head in her hands, not knowing how much time had passed or how long she sat there.

Eventually, she knew she had to move. She must find Alan. What if Maria tried to tackle him about her crazy suspicions? He would need Jen's support. She crossed the empty hall to look out of the front door and there was no sign of Alan or Maria or Graham. She hesitated, unsure what to do next.

Perhaps the house was getting to her, and not in a good way. She wasn't thinking straight any more and this was Dorothy's home; perhaps this was how Dorothy had felt. All too easy to become overwhelmed by hopelessness, with the woods beckoning and knowing constantly that the pool was there. It was waiting, Jen knew. Waiting to bring release.

No. She made herself snap out of the clouding despair and looked at her watch. At last, time to be rounding everyone up. No more surprises. She went outside, past the open garage. Something out here wasn't right. She frowned, unable to work it out. There was an empty space in the garage next to Graham's car. Alan had gone. She stared at the gap and the hard grey floor.

This was so like him, setting off in a rush, without thinking. She just hoped he had taken his full quota of passengers. She didn't hear Graham coming until he spoke. 'By the way, Alan's gone. He asked me to tell you. He had to dash off. I think he got a text message.'

'Oh, I see.' Relief. Her knees almost buckled. Nothing to do with Maria accusing him of anything. 'Fair enough. Did he take anyone with him?' She was thinking only of the numbers.

Graham put a hand on her arm, his voice gentle. 'Maria, I'm afraid.'

Jen couldn't stop the angry gasp. 'I might have known. Can't he see what she's trying to do?' Although now she was hardly certain herself. Was Maria trying to incriminate Alan or ensnare him? You could hardly trust anything

Maria said. Graham said nothing, waiting politely. She made a huge effort to pull herself together. 'Never mind. We're almost ready to go. We won't be far behind them.' Assuming they had returned to Birkedge. But face that when it comes to it.

'I've checked the woods myself for stragglers,' Graham said helpfully. 'Thought it would save you a job.'

Jen smiled gratefully. Already there were figures sitting on the coach. 'Alan's left already,' Nelly told her. 'He didn't stop. He came driving straight out of the garage and off.'

'Yes, I know about that, thanks. Graham told me.' She bit her lip. 'And that means we'll be short of seats. Do you think you could squash up with someone else?'

'Maria was with him, I saw the orange coat. Yes, I don't mind sharing. I'm sure we can squeeze in at the back. Lucky I'm skin and bone, isn't it and not like some, Dora?'

Everyone else was there, right on

time — except Erica. 'Has anyone seen her?' Jen said wearily. Shaking of heads. 'I expect she'll be in one of the bathrooms. She usually is. I'll go and get her.'

The driver leaned forward as she passed him. 'I can't stay longer than half past. I've got that evening booking to get back for.'

'There's no problem. We'll soon find her.' A short discussion and she, Graham and Simon split up to perform a lightning search. Jen took the house. No sign of her mother and the upstairs bathroom was locked again. And the small jar in the bedroom was empty. Heaven knew where Maria had put the key but Erica couldn't be in there.

Back to the coach and Simon and Graham were returning from their different directions, alone. Jen's heart sank. How could Erica do this to her? She made a decision. 'It's all right. You can all set off on the coach and I'll stay behind until she turns up. You can be in charge, Harold and I'll phone Alan and ask him to come back for us.' Would that be a good idea? Perhaps they should get a taxi. There was too much going on here that she didn't understand. This might be the last place Alan should be. She knew in one revealing moment that whatever he'd done made no difference. She still loved him and would always love him; she must protect Alan before anything else.

Graham said, 'Don't worry about any of that. I can run you and Erica back.'

'Of course. Thanks, Graham.' That would solve everything.

* * *

It was a disaster. Graham had opened the envelope smiling nervously at his mother and then stared in disbelief. Since then he had shut himself in his bedroom. It was the end of Dorothy's hopes for her quiet and clever younger son. But it was Alan who sorted everything out. He phoned Dorothy that evening to tell her he had found a flat in Chiswick to go with his new job.

'That's wonderful, Alan.' She kept her voice steady and calm.

'What's the matter?'

'Graham didn't get the grades he needed to do history at Manchester. I can't understand it. He worked so hard.'

'That was today, wasn't it? The A-level results? I'd forgotten.' Alan paused. 'Perhaps he was worrying too much. And it hit him hard when Frank died.'

'But that was a while ago.' As if yesterday, to her. But not, surely, to Graham?

'I know. I thought he was OK with it by now. It was just something he said, only this summer. Anyway, I'll think of something. Don't worry.'

And in no time it seemed, Alan had found a degree course in North London, actually begging for students. London? So far away? Manchester would have been so convenient. They had worked out that Graham would be able to come home every night. But if this was his only chance, as Alan seemed to think, she couldn't stand in his way. 'It sounds marvellous.' It was always the same with Alan, rush, rush, rush. But she couldn't take the risk of Graham losing this opportunity.

She had to be brave in front of the boys but once the day of parting had arrived and she waved Alan's red Metro away, there was no need to hide her grief. Not more pain. The loss was a great dark hole inside her, sucking her in.

Alan phoned her when they arrived to give quick, comforting words and hinting at a new project and a surprise before he had to hurry off somewhere. Another of his many schemes, Dorothy supposed.

Graham, bless him, phoned her every night and with her younger son the conversation was easier, more relaxed. 'Are you all right, Mum?'

'Yes, I'm finding plenty to do. There's so much to see to in the garden at this time of year. The hypericum is flowering at last and the herb garden is healthy. I'm taking great care of your special plants.'

'That's good. And listen, I haven't any lectures this week. I can come home for the weekend on Friday.'

'Graham! I never thought I'd see you so soon. And what about Alan?' Graham told her he was very busy with his new job, working all hours. 'Never mind. The main thing is that I shall be seeing you.'

Every minute dragged until she saw him again. She jumped out of the car and threw her arms round him in the station car park. This is true happiness, she thought. Isn't it? 'Oh, Graham, it's so lovely to see you.' Now that the anticipated moment had come, it wasn't quite what she had been expecting. Already there was a subtle difference in him. He was growing apart from her. She had a dull grey feeling she couldn't explain. And a dread of that other moment, on

Sunday, when he would have to leave her again.

But there was no need to worry about that. This was Friday and the golden hours lay before them. She cooked for him, they lunched at the Laurence Arms, he admired the garden and she sat and watched as he sorted a few more items he thought he would need.

Dorothy didn't sleep on the Saturday night. She wanted to cherish the knowledge that Graham was asleep in the room next door, not wasting a minute. When the sun rose, she crept into his room and smiled down at him, the fair hair tangled untidily. He looked so young.

She saw herself in the full-length mirror, wearing her pale dressing gown and looking down at this beauteous young knight. Like a stylised composition of a Pre-Raphaelite painting. Except that her face was haggard and her eyes were sad. She was doing it again, immersing herself in self-pity.

With no thought of how Graham would hate to leave her in this state. This wouldn't do. A quick bath and some fresh air might help. When she was dressed, she would go for a walk and sit by the pool. Sitting there always calmed her.

October sunshine chilled the blood. She found herself thinking about Frank. Poor Frank. He had loved her in his way. She could see that now.

She had come out here into the trees to steady herself but as she stood by the pool, her new resolutions wavered and she was tempted. The water could give her more than a temporary calm. Had she been drawn here for this very reason? The pool was offering the long-term solution of consolation and oblivion.

Death or life? The dark ripples seemed to be offering a choice. She had been so happy here once, on that last day with Frank. As she looked down into the water, once more she could see two figures reflected there. She stared down, daring to hope. Smiling down to where the movement had come and gone.

This must be a sign, a message of apology and encouragement from Frank. Perhaps she had learned to forgive after all.

The pool had offered her a choice and she had chosen. Chosen to face up to this new stage in her life and accept the new challenges. She shook her head at herself, awed at just how seriously she had considered stepping down into the darkness of the water. That would have been so wrong. She knew now that she would go on to accept what life had to offer, pleasure and pain, light and dark. She would wave Graham away with a smile.

But the fist between her shoulder blades was quick and hard and her hands thrashed at the air as she fell.

12

'Erica may have wandered back to the Hall,' Graham said.

Simon shook his head. 'I don't think so. I would have seen her. That's why I've been hanging around all afternoon, making sure that didn't happen.'

Although the two men were civil, even pleasant, with each other, there seemed to be a feeling of tension between them. Jen thought, but so what? She just wanted to get on with this and get away, to follow Alan and Maria. Unless? No, there was no possibility whatsoever that Erica would have left with them.

Simon shrugged. 'I'll go back to the Hall if that's what you want.' He strode away.

'Otherwise,' Graham said, 'I'm not sure what to suggest.'

Jen pushed her hair back behind her

ears. 'I suggest we go over the whole place again, inside and out, the two of us together. Very slowly and investigating each corner.'

They began with the barn and the outbuildings. 'Nothing, you see,' Graham said. 'And those doors are all padlocked.'

'Do you have the keys? I know it sounds silly but I have to be certain.'

He nodded. 'I'll get them. I won't be long. Wait here.'

Jen looked round the courtyard. At the far corner, a narrow gap led behind the barn to a wilderness of trees and undergrowth. Worth checking. Jen walked along the side of the barn as Graham was hurrying out of the kitchen doorway. He called, 'That's only an old cold store. We always keep the door barred. I can't see why Erica would have gone round there.'

But someone had. Jen picked her way through crushed nettles. The door was held shut from the outside by a wooden stake in two metal hasps. She called back, 'I can hear something!' She unthreaded the stake, pulled at the handle and staggered back as the door was pushed violently from the inside. 'Mother! What on earth are you doing in there?'

Erica was blinking into the light like a confused owl. Her raincoat was grey with dust and old cobwebs. 'I don't know what happened. Graham said there were some of his paintings stored in here. I wanted to see more of his work. You said I could, Graham.'

'Yes, I did. But not in here. They're in that outhouse over on the other side.' Graham was panting a little. 'Erica, I'm so sorry. You must have misunderstood. I should have come with you. And somehow this door must have stuck.

Stuck? Jen thought. It was barred. But that didn't matter now. She turned to Erica, annoyed that her mother should have got herself into this situation but relieved too. Although now Alan and Maria were heaven knew where and she was left here. She held out her arms as Erica swayed. 'Just thank goodness you're safe.'

'I know what must have happened,' Graham said. 'I can't apologise enough. It would be the boy from the village who comes in to help with the garden. He's supposed to check all the doors are locked and bolted before he goes home. I'll have a word with him.'

Strange that they hadn't noticed him. But perhaps he'd been told to keep out of the way. 'Come on, we must get you home.'

'Bring her inside and let her sit down first,' Graham said. 'You've had a nasty shock, Erica, but it's all right now. Come and have a rest and a hot drink.'

They took Erica into the parlour and Graham brought her a cupful of something that he said would be good for shock. 'Only elderberry and echinacea and one or two other things. You can have a nice hot cup of tea too. And I'm going to drive you back so there's no rush.' Erica was sipping cautiously. 'And Jen's going to phone and leave a message for Alan to put his mind at rest.'

'Thanks, I was forgetting about that. Ah, my phone isn't showing any reception. Can I use your landline?'

'In the hall. Help yourself.'

There was nothing from Alan's mobile either but then, he would still be driving. She would leave a message on their home phone. In front of her on the old-fashioned wrought iron telephone shelf, there was a glass dish containing a key. She knew as she left her message that it was the bathroom key.

Why on earth had Maria left it here? That was so careless. In such a hurry to rush off with Alan that she couldn't be bothered to cover her tracks. Graham would be sure to notice. She must put it back.

Jen put the key in her pocket as Graham came through the hall. 'You'll have coffee, will you, Jen? Milk and no sugar, wasn't it? I'm doing Erica's tea first.'

She followed him as far as the stairs and called after him, not wanting to tell the lie to his face. 'I think I left my comb in the bedroom. I let Maria borrow it. OK if I pop and get it?' Her face was hot as she mounted the stairs.

The key was hard and cold in her fingers. Perhaps she wouldn't put it back in the bedroom straightaway. Just a quick look, that was all. Had Maria found something in here that she'd had to tell Alan about — and urgently? If so, Jen needed to know what it was. Without giving herself the chance to object, Jen turned the key again and quietly twisted the doorknob. The door opened easily and she slid through the gap and looked round. Too dark to see anything. She closed the door behind her and switched on the light.

The room was packed. There was too much to take in all at once. A pile of bedding was trailed and heaped across the toilet, up and over the washbasin. The small window was obscured by a number of paintings propped against the glass. That was why the room was so dark. And Graham must mix his paints here because there were red splashes on the white ceramic, wet stains on the white tiled walls.

There were more paintings lined up against the foot of the bath. All portraits and all in Graham's photographic style, accurate to the point of obsession. She recognised Lisa again and also a woman with sad eyes, who did indeed resemble the Celia Laurence portrait, and who must be Dorothy. And a younger, paler Maria with long straight hair. There were only two men: Alan and Simon Parkestone.

Jen thought, they're very good. But nothing here to send Maria hurrying home in triumph. And nothing, thank goodness, that could incriminate Alan in the slightest.

There was a second row of paintings behind the first. Graham had said he was going to do one of her, hadn't he? Would it be here? She put out a hand to the nearest one, the picture of Lisa, and frowned as she pulled it away.

In the painting revealed underneath, the technique seemed quite different. As if Graham had turned to abstract art. Because the face was still Lisa's but swollen and misshapen. The flesh tones were overlaid with a dark palette of blues and blacks, bloated and bruised. She let the frame fall and stepped back. No, not abstract. It was Lisa in death. A caricature of that vital, acerbic face. She flicked along the row and they were all the same. Horrible. Particularly the one of Alan. But why had Graham done this? Alan wasn't dead. None of these people were dead. She put the back of her hand to her mouth, turned too fast and almost fell into the pile of bedding.

A sienna-coloured elderdown fell away and Maria's body lolled back against her. Blood in the dark hair, her features puffed. A hand slopped into the washbasin and water splashed out over Jen's feet.

The outside world swayed while Jen stood still. Maria couldn't be here. She was in the car with Alan.

Alan, Jen thought.

Alan had killed Maria like he killed Lisa and his own mother. It hadn't been Maria in the car, only the orange fleece. By the time the car left, Maria hadn't been wearing the fleece. Alan hadn't rushed off with Maria; he had been fleeing from Maria and what he had done. Driving away from this crumpled travesty, here in the bathroom.

The moment expanded and she was inside a vast hollow, crying out in the dark. Unable to stop loving Alan, even though he had done this horrible thing. It's all right, Alan, she thought. I shan't tell anyone. No one need ever know.

What was she thinking of? She was wasting time. Kiss of life. No, hands-only CPR. There could still be a chance. She began trying to lift Maria away from the basin, trying not to hurt her and trying to remember the First Aid course she'd attended. ABC. Signs of life. No, nothing. For someone so thin, Maria was heavy now and she slid through Jen's hands and thudded down onto the sheets. Jen knew she would have to get help.

A sound came from the doorway behind her and she was hot with relief. Graham. He would get an ambulance and he would help her to protect Alan. 'It's Maria. She's — had some kind of terrible accident.'

He stepped forward. 'What are you trying to do? She's dead. It's no use. I'm sorry.'

'I think she must have slipped. And I think it must have been Alan.' She was shaking her head as she spoke and the rest of herself followed on. Her whole body was shaking with denial.

'Why would Alan do that?' Graham put an arm around her. His voice was calm — and that was what they needed. She was grateful for that.

'Don't you see? Because Maria knew he had killed Lisa. And there were so many little things pointing to it but I didn't believe Maria. I thought she was

254

just being friendly at first and then I thought she was trying to get Alan back. I didn't like her. But I didn't want anything like this to happen. I didn't want her dead.' She wasn't sure she was making sense and she had to convince him. Because any moment now he would stop her and insist on ringing the police and she couldn't allow that to happen. She needed to be certain about Alan, one way or the other. She needed time. It looked so bad and the police would arrest him. 'I have to get in touch with Alan. I want him to get away.'

'I see. You must love him very much.'

'Yes, of course I do. I'm sure he never meant to do this. She must have slipped somehow.'

'Perhaps we don't need to ring the police. I could take you and Erica home and you could say nothing and we could allow events to take their course. I could conceal the body in the woods. I should think she wouldn't be missed for some time.'

'You would do that for Alan?' Jen's

eyes were watering. She blinked, quickly.

'I'm sure he'd do the same for me. I'll see to everything. Wash your hands and come downstairs and I'll run you both home straightaway.' He was gripping her elbow with a wiry strength.

She glanced back at Maria. 'Perhaps we should cover her up.'

'No.' His voice was sharp and she looked at him, surprised. He smiled back at her. 'You've done enough. Come away.' He led her into the main bedroom, opening the doors so she could wash the blood from her hands. 'I'll leave you to it.'

She stood at the sink, still numb with shock. The water splashed and ran and her mind cleared with the cleansing soap. Graham. The dead faces in the portraits. What kind of mind would paint dead faces like that? Still-life, still-death. Sick and morbid. Graham, not Alan. Why had she ever thought it would be Alan? Because that was what Maria had wanted her to think. Playing games with Jen's mind. But all the time, Maria had been endangering herself, never realising what the consequences might be.

Yes, Graham had killed Maria. He had been so calm and cool just now. An unnatural reaction. Her hands began to shake and she scrubbed them with the towel. Not Alan. Thank God, thank God. But where was Alan? Why had he driven off so suddenly if not with Maria?

And somehow she had to get herself and Erica safely away from here. Perhaps if she could seem to go along with the story Graham had invented, they might be safe enough for now. Don't, on any account, say anything to upset him and disturb his plan. When she could eventually get to the police, they would sort all this out. But for now, one step at a time.

Her neck prickled and she turned round. Graham was behind her again, watching her. She hadn't heard him returning. She must not allow her thoughts to show in her face. He said, 'I came up to tell you that Erica is fast asleep. She's worn out.'

'Oh, dear. Because we should be getting back.' She was thinking quickly as she followed him down the stairs. Perhaps leaving wasn't going to be as simple as she had hoped.

'No, she needs to sleep.' He turned into the kitchen, leaving her in the hall.

The phone, Jen thought. Should she risk dialling 999? She stared at the wrought iron shelf. The phone was no longer there. It was only minutes ago that she had used it.

Graham was behind her, a mug in each hand. 'She will sleep well now. You see, I put something in her herbal drink to help Erica to sleep. Something a bit stronger than valerian, which is the usual of course.'

'Oh, did you?' Jen was still thrown off-balance by the phone. Why had Graham unplugged it? And now — what was he saying? A cold trickle slid down her back.

'Don't worry. I know what I'm doing. I've come a long way since I first heard about plants and their uses.' He made a self-deprecating gesture, hunching a shoulder. 'Chocolates indeed! Downright foolishness. But I was young and lacking in judgement. Yes, I feel that a timely doze is just what's needed. Otherwise, you know, Erica would be bouncing in and interrupting our chat. I dislike being interrupted, especially by someone like her. She is a most annoying woman, isn't she? My mother wouldn't have cared for her at all. And yet I mustn't be too hard on her because she's served her purpose today. I knew you would stay behind to look for her. I knew you would be a caring and dutiful daughter. Filial devotion was always my aim in life and I empathise so readily when I see those qualities.'

She smiled doubtfully. Fear crawled along the back of her neck. Think. She must keep playing him along. And he must know she had noticed the missing phone. She said lightly, 'And I suppose that's why you unplugged the phone too? To avoid disturbing her. That was very thoughtful.'

He smiled back. 'Exactly. And we don't need it for now, do we? It's so much easier nowadays, with that convenient little socket. Although when Simon tried to frighten my mother, he had to cut the wires. Yes, it's history repeating itself in a way. But I've forgiven him for that. He was only doing what his father made him do. Anyway, I don't intend that you should be frightened.' He was standing too close to her. She resisted the urge to step back. He was holding the coffee mugs between them and she could feel the heat on the backs of her hands. 'You're not frightened, are you, Jen? There's no need.'

She made herself smile again. 'No, I'm fine.' Did he have any intention of ever driving them back? Perhaps she could get hold of his car keys. But Jen couldn't do anything with Erica asleep and vulnerable.

'Come outside. We'll sit in the herb garden.' He gestured for her to go first, round the side of the house. She made herself avoid a longing glance across to the garage. He was too clever; he must not guess her thoughts. The herb garden was warm and inviting with a wooden bench catching the evening sun. 'There. You need to rest too, I know.' He passed a mug to her as they sat down. 'Take it.'

She took it doubtfully. Was there something in her drink as well? 'You're very kind but I don't need anything to help me sleep.'

He laughed out loud. 'No, no. You're missing the point. Erica has to be out of the way whereas you have become very important. This is all working out so well.' He gave a small sigh of satisfaction. 'You have some days in life, don't you, when in spite of setbacks, you can overcome all obstacles as if inspired?'

'In what way?' If she could just encourage him to keep talking while she tried to work out what to do, the sooner they might have a chance of making their escape. At least there seemed to be none of the anger he had directed at Lisa and Maria. His manner to Jen was friendly and approving and she must keep it that way. But she still didn't have the least idea what he was talking about.

'Let me explain. This is all for the best. It will be the end of so much pain and suffering which began with my mother — but for a long time, I couldn't see what she wanted and what the pool wanted. Everyone always thinks Alan is the strong one, you know. But I am the one who sees what needs to be done and takes action. I killed the rabbit. Alan couldn't do it. Dad shouted at him but he was shivering and crying too much. He dropped the hammer. So I did it. And it was so easy.' He was shaking his head. 'All that fuss.'

Yes, Alan. Of course. Jen said, 'I

expect Alan will probably come back to look for us anyway, when he sees we weren't on the coach. It won't take him long.'

'No, no, no. You're missing the point — again.' He sounded amused rather than annoyed. 'Alan had to be here. Mum was so close to Alan. She would want him with her more than anyone else.'

Jen's hands were cold. A coldness that was spreading inside her. She paused to drink, trying to make sense of what Graham had just said. 'So where is Alan?'

'He's in the willows, beyond the pool.' Graham's voice was unbelievably matter-of-fact. 'We took the car along the lane and parked in one of the tracks, under the trees. I told him you'd hurt your leg and I was wearing the orange fleece so anyone glancing at the car would think Alan had left with Maria. It was very easy. I wanted him to walk to the pool before I hit him. That's the whole point of the triple sacrifice.

The chosen person goes willingly, even joyfully. Mum walked there of her own accord. I knew what I had to do when I followed her. Unfair that life brought her so much unhappiness. She couldn't cope with the pain. I was the only one who could help her.'

This isn't happening, Jen thought. I'm not hearing this. Her brain was frantically seeking and rejecting possibilities at breakneck speed. 'Is Alan all right?'

'I haven't dealt with him properly yet if that's what you mean. Far too many people crashing about. And I didn't want to do it in a hurry; that would spoil it. No, I can go back whenever I choose. I bound him so that's no problem. It will be done properly and well and when we're ready. You can help — because you understand about the joy and the acquiescence, don't you? Mum will be so pleased.'

I could run, Jen thought but it was unlikely that she would get far and it would mean leaving Erica here on her own with him. And where could she go? The Hall and the village were both too distant. But at least Alan was alive. If she could believe anything that the sadly deluded Graham was telling her. And for how long? Simon, she thought suddenly. What about him?

'Don't worry about Simon. He understands me. He always has done.'

How had he done that? Had her lips unconsciously formed Simon's name? But would Simon understand so well if he knew that a death portrait of himself was in Graham's bathroom? Simon was a possibility but she wouldn't rely on him. Perhaps she could hit Graham with something. She glanced carefully round the garden. No stray tools or even any loose stones. The garden was as tidy as the house.

Keep him talking. There was nothing else to do. If she could understand these strange ideas, she might be able to talk him out of them. 'This is all very interesting. I would like to understand too. Why don't you tell me all about it?'

She hoped she sounded convincing.

Graham leaned forward earnestly. 'You've no idea how much I've longed to do that. I wanted to tell Lisa so badly. But she had no time to listen to me. She was too wrapped up in herself.' He set his empty mug down on the bench and sharply slapped his hand onto his knee. Jen jumped and her coffee splattered her arm. He said, 'How could my mother go on living in such pain? I heard her weeping every night and the sound crept through the whole house. And I knew that she was alone because of me.'

'But it's natural to grow up and leave home.'

'She shouldn't have been left on her own when I went to university. We'd planned it all. But I failed my exams. I had too much to cope with that last year. Too much on my mind. I couldn't work. Couldn't even think. And Alan realised what was happening to me. He found me a place in London; Mum and I thought it was because there was no alternative. We were swept along — you know how Alan is — and I accepted because I thought there was no choice. I never realised there was a rational explanation. Alan never offered one and I didn't think to ask.' He stopped and took a breath, throwing his head back. 'Forgive me. I'm trying to say I was to blame for my mother's misery. If only Frank had still been there to care for her, everything would have been all right. I'm sure Frank did love her even though he had been so devious and manipulative. Otherwise he could have been much more ruthless.'

'I see.' Jen's chest felt tight. Somehow she must get to Alan. Even if she could knock Graham out, would she be able to find Alan on her own? She had to find Alan and set him free. She couldn't trust Graham's casual reassurance about not hitting him too hard. Graham was no longer in touch with reality. He might agree to take her to Alan but would she only be endangering him further? She didn't want to accept it but all this talk about sacrifices and being together with Dorothy could only have one meaning.

He said regretfully, 'I never meant to kill Frank.'

She was jolted out of her thoughts. 'What?'

'The chocolates were meant for Simon. Just to make him ill, that's all. I never thought he wouldn't eat them himself. I didn't know he would take them to Frank, in hospital. I must have overdone it. For a man with a suspect heart, the dosage must have been fatal.' He rested his elbows on his knees, shaking his head.

'You mean, you put something in them? But — you don't have any evidence that the chocolates had any adverse effect on Frank, do you? Let alone kill him.'

'I knew. Mum said she'd seen the chocolate box in the hospital. That was when I knew.'

Jen almost felt sorry for him. In this at least. 'And all this time, you've been blaming yourself? I'm not convinced you had anything to do with Frank's death. You were just a boy, messing about with — what? Essence of foxglove or something? I can't see that you could have killed him.'

'I didn't mess about. If I tackled anything, I did it well. Always. I had to if I wanted to impress my father.'

Jen stared at him, not sure what she could say about his father.

Graham was folding his hands around each other. 'It was my fault that Mum was never going to be happy again. That was why I had to do it.' He rested his head on his hands, covering his eyes. 'And I was so much happier within myself, knowing that Mum was at rest. But I couldn't make Alan understand. I tried to tell him what I'd done and he wouldn't talk about it. I didn't know whether he understood or not. And when I started teaching and met Lisa, Alan and I drifted apart even more. He disliked her at first.'

Jen felt it wasn't a good idea to dwell

on the matter of Alan and Lisa even though Graham had already told her he hadn't resented their affair. And she still didn't understand half of what he was telling her and wasn't sure whether it was getting her anywhere. Perhaps they should move on a little. She decided to try a different approach. 'I'm sure your mother is at peace now, as you say. It sounds as if you've been bottling your feelings up for years. If you and I and Alan could have a long talk together, that would make you feel happier within yourself.'

He wasn't listening. His voice rose. 'I didn't set out to kill Lisa. Don't think that. Even though she was having an affair with Alan and she was suffering from depression like my mother. I knew, I just knew I couldn't stand much more of it. I couldn't go through all that again.'

'No. Of course you couldn't.' She had only made things worse; she was way out of her depth here.

'And killing Lisa was the last thing I

intended. It was her idea, her fault. As we left the hotel, she was driving — and shouting at me as she drove. She said she would leave me and I said I wished she would. She stopped the car on the bridge and I got out and so did she. She was shrieking and screaming. She said if I didn't listen to her, she would kill herself. And she climbed up onto the parapet. Just to frighten me. I'd seen it before. So many times. This time I thought, yes. The answer to everything. So I pushed her.'

Jen nodded. 'I see.' There didn't seem to be anything else to say.

'And that marked the liberation, more than anything else. From then on, Mum was inside my head, leading me and inspiring me. I knew that the whole family must be brought together as she would have wanted. I only thought about Alan and myself to begin with but when he married you, that opened another possibility.'

She opened her mouth and decided she didn't want to know what he meant. He was obviously waiting for a response. She said, in desperation, 'How did Maria fit in to all this?'

'Yes, you're thinking that Maria is a distraction. But Mum was always so fond of her. She was so disappointed when that romance came to nothing. I hadn't planned Maria's death, but I didn't need to. She too brought it upon herself. And everything has come together better than I could ever have hoped.'

'But supposing you've got it wrong? And this isn't what your mother would have wanted at all?'

'It's taken so long. I knew what I had to do but after Lisa died, Alan was avoiding me. I wanted the next steps to take place here because of the pool and its sacred connections. Because my mother was always so interested in my researches.' He laughed and the sound was young and joyful. 'It's ironic. I tried so hard to get Alan's attention — and yours. I even sent messages from Lisa's phone.'

'That was you? And you sent them to Alan too?' How could anyone do that?

'And you both ignored me. But I'm glad now that I had to wait. Mum knew best. I couldn't believe it when Alan phoned and I saw how you would all be arriving here voluntarily. As if fated. The willing chosen, arriving for the sacrifice. Mum's guidance obviously.' He frowned. 'But I didn't intend your mother to be a part of it, even though she'd managed to work herself into the plan, uninvited. However, it will be managed. Although she doesn't warrant a place in the pool, I'm afraid. Not like you, Jen.'

His words had become almost hypnotic. She jerked in shock. 'What? No, I don't think so. I'm sure I don't deserve a place either.'

He took her wrists and pulled her to her feet. The mugs fell and shattered. His smile held a solemn joy. 'Come with me.'

13

Jen walked into the trees with Graham gripping her arms. She could do nothing. And didn't want to until she knew where Alan was. Graham said, 'You're like her, you know. You have the same large sad eyes.'

'Your mother. Yes, I suppose so. But I'm not sad.'

'And that was why Alan was first attracted to you, showing wisdom in his choice. That was my mistake because Lisa was nothing like our mother.' He was silent and she was aware of the sound of their footsteps and the rustling of the branches as they brushed past. 'We all need someone to talk to in depth. Someone we can trust completely. Lisa could never give me that.'

'Yes, that's how it is with Alan and me. We're very happy. As we are.'

'I expected to be punished after I

helped Mum to die. I told Alan knowing he would do the right thing and I wouldn't have to make that decision. But nothing happened. He didn't tell anyone or do anything. He just got himself transferred to Buckinghamshire and I hardly saw him.'

Jen couldn't let that pass. 'I'm sure Alan's silence wouldn't mean he approved of what you had done. You were his brother and the only person he had left and I don't suppose he knew what to do for the best.'

He stopped, putting a hand beneath her chin and tilting her face towards the sunlight. She blinked, protecting her eyes. He said, 'Don't try to undermine my purpose. When you know something is so right, nothing can distract.' He released her face and pulled her onwards. 'And even though you and Alan betrayed me today by trying to steal my home, I can forgive you both. Because of course, after today, it won't matter.'

A relief in a way to talk about

something ordinary. 'I'm so sorry about the house sale. We should have told you straightaway. As soon as Alan made the decision. But he thought you understood this was only a temporary arrangement. You said so yourself. A temporary bolt-hole.'

'Yes. Alan thinks about me a lot and always has done. It's only a pity that he gets things so wrong. As before, when he thought I would be better in London, well away from here — but see what that led to? And it wasn't necessary. During that first week in London, he told me what he'd done and why, persuading me it was for the best. I hadn't understood. And neither had he. Apparently he thought Simon was an undesirable influence. That he wanted to be too close to me. But left to himself, Simon was soft and harmless. He only pretends to be ruthless and decisive. I had to teach him.' He sighed. 'Alan was far too late if his intention was removing me from Simon. The whole thing became one huge muddle. Alan only wanted to help but this is what happens when you try to interfere in other people's lives.'

The sun had gone and the wind was rising once more in little trickling gusts. They seemed to have been walking forever. 'You understand sorrow, Jen. That's the point. I feel your sorrow within myself.'

The pool lay ahead. Her feet slipped on smooth stone. She said, 'Where's Alan? You promised to bring me to him.'

'I have. I couldn't leave him out in the open, could I? Not with Simon mooching around. Sometimes he gets things wrong too.' He pulled her away from the stones, kicking at the under-growth. And Alan was there, lying on his side with his hands behind him. There was leaf mould mixed with the blood on his forehead. Jen dropped onto her knees as her heart lurched, putting an ear to the white face. 'Alan, can you hear me?'

Graham said conversationally, 'It's

difficult to judge when you hit someone like that. A messy way of doing things because you don't have the control. Not like the herbs. You know where you are with them. Everything can be measured so exactly.' He gave a short grunt of amusement. 'But you all believed me, didn't you? You all thought it was Maria in the car with Alan.'

Alan was still breathing. Thank God. Stilted, gasping breaths but his chest was moving. He was all right.

'Yes,' Graham said, 'I want him to come round. I didn't have time to explain the privilege of the sacrifice to him. And of course this is actually more of an appeasement than a sacrifice. A peace-making. You understand, don't you, Jen? I think you're the only one who does.'

'Yes.' Just agree with him. There was no hope of talking him out of this. No chance of getting him away from this obsessive recurring theme. Alan was alive but unconscious; there could be no help from him. She looked back along the way they had come. Were any of those stones loose? But they looked too big to grasp, even if they had been. She had to choose something she could manage. She had to protect Alan and she would only have one chance.

Graham was pulling her up. 'My mother has told me that you are to be the first. Here, see. This is where you are to stand. This is where my mother stood, looking down.' There was a caress in his voice.

She forced her limbs to relax. 'How is the ceremony to be a triple death, Graham? Did Dorothy have a triple death?' There was a short stubby branch on the other side of the pool. Alan's branch, the impromptu walking stick, flung down in anger hours ago.

'No. I told you. That came out of the blue. I hadn't thought it through.' He sounded disappointed. 'But I have a stone and a cord ready and there will be no mistake now. I owe her that.' He dropped Jen's arms and was feeling within his pockets.

One chance. It was all she had and all she could think of. Jen stepped back, lunged forwards and pushed him, with all her strength. But his hand snapped back to her in some kind of a reflex action; he grasped her sleeve and they fell together.

The splash stung her face, her hands. She ducked away from him and struck out, trying to swim. But they were too near the edge and her feet struck the bottom, confusing her. She had never known water this cold. It froze her limbs, making movement almost impossible.

Graham was recovering from the first shock and gaining a foothold. He was standing, not more than a couple of feet away from her. Now he was striding and splashing after her. The hood of her cagoule was filled with a great weight of water. She shook it out, screaming, 'Help me.' A futile instinct when she knew there was no one to hear.

Graham was shouting, 'Let me help you. It's all right. It's all over.'

Jen fought her way to the other side, sure that at any moment she would feel his hands gripping her neck. Half swimming in the centre, remembering how someone had said it was deep in the middle. Behind her, Graham swore as he sank, forgetting about the depth. Only briefly but it gave her a few precious moments of advantage. She clutched at the stones but there was no chance of climbing out. They were too slippery and there was no time to try and hoist herself up. But her reaching fingers met Alan's discarded branch. She clasped at it with both hands and turned to face him.

He was right behind her, smiling. Jen raised her arms over her head, leaning back against the stones, seeking their strength. And brought the branch down with all the force she could. She heard the crack as the branch hit his head. He staggered back and she struck out at him again and again and at last he fell back, arms circling in an effort to regain his balance. And was still.

Gasping, she knew she now had the time she needed to heave herself up onto the stones. Her arms found a further strength she had not known she possessed. She was panting painfully. All her body wanted to do was to collapse onto the hard flat stones and rest. But she couldn't. She had to go to Alan. She staggered into the bushes where he was lying. 'Alan,' she called. 'It's all right. I'm here.'

She pulled at the cords round his wrists and was only making them tighter. All the time she was glancing back at the pool, expecting to see a vengeful Graham coming round and surging out. Take it slowly. Be calm. She would have to go back to the house for something to cut them. A knife, scissors. She cast another sideways glance at the pool. No movement. Not yet. She didn't know how much time she had. But when he got out, Graham wouldn't go for Alan. Not straightaway. He would come after her, wouldn't he? She had to take that chance. What else could she do?

She whispered, 'I won't be long, Alan. I promise.' She began to run back along the path and a tall thin figure was coming towards her. She stopped. Simon Parkestone. Could she trust him? What was it Graham had said? That Simon knew what he had planned. There was no way of avoiding him. He had seen her now.

He said, 'What's the matter? Is something wrong?'

The words would hardly come out. She was gulping with fear. 'Graham attacked me. He's in the pool. I — had to hit him with a stick.'

He nodded, his face blank.

For the first time, she realised that Graham should have been coming after her by now. 'I think he should have got out himself out. But he hasn't.'

Simon Parkestone sighed. 'You go back to the house. I'll see to Graham. And ring for an ambulance if he needs one.'

'But — there's Alan. I need a knife or

something. Alan's tied up.'

He muttered something that sounded like, 'Can it get any worse?' He was delving in an inside pocket and produced a penknife and a mobile phone, following her round the pool as he summoned the emergency services. She avoided looking at Graham. She was beginning to have a heavy feeling of dread in the pit of her stomach. But her companion spared the pool no more than a brief glance. His face was giving no indication of his feelings as he knelt beside Alan and began sawing at the damp ropes.

She said, 'I can do this. You see to — Graham.'

He ignored her. Jen hardly waited for the threads to part before she was pulling the twine away and rubbing Alan's wrists. 'No,' Simon said. 'Splash some water on his face. I'll do his feet.' Still in the same dull expressionless voice.

Something didn't seem quite right but she obeyed, taking off her cagoule and using the hood for the water. Only looking at the edge of the pool where she knelt and no further. And as the water splashed onto his face, Alan groaned. Jen's hands were shaking with relief. He groaned again and coughed, opening his eyes. 'Jen. You're all right.' She put her arms around him. He tried to sit and collapsed against her.

'He's OK.' Simon Parkestone stood up, slowly. There was no sense of urgency. He walked away from them, back to the pool. Graham was floating now, within reach. Simon Parkestone leaned over and took hold of the nearest arm, pulling him in.

Reluctantly, Jen said, 'I'll help you.' Was he dead? And so easily? It didn't seem possible. Yet he wasn't moving. Was he even breathing? If he was alive, he was dangerous. 'He's murdered Maria. She's in the bathroom.'

Simon nodded as he took off his jacket. He eased himself down into the water and waded in. Jen bit her lips together and helped by pulling as

Simon heaved. Graham seemed incredibly heavy. But at last he was lying on the ground beside her. Simon climbed out. They turned him over. One hand slapped onto the stones, a wet fish sound. Simon said, 'I might have known.' She didn't know whether this was a delayed response to her telling him about Maria. Or to everything. She didn't ask.

Behind her, Alan was still coughing, sitting with his head and arms resting onto his bent knees. She didn't know whether he could see them or even knew what had happened to Graham. Jen felt as if she had been asleep and was only just waking up. She said, 'Shouldn't we try the kiss of life? It may not be too late.' She might have been able to save Maria. She could have tried. Graham had stopped her.

Simon said firmly, 'I'm afraid it is too late. Far too late.'

'But you rang 999? They're on their way? I think Alan might need an ambulance as well.' He had seemed to be having a conversation with someone. 'How did your phone work here? Mine doesn't.'

'You need to be on the right network.' He jerked his head to one side. 'See to Alan. He should be in the house.'

Jen was glad to obey. Alan was still sitting there, staring at the ground, saying nothing. After his first agonised question, he seemed disorientated. She said, 'Can you walk? Simon will stay with Graham. I'll explain. We'll go to the house and wait for the ambulance there.' She helped him up and by leaning against her, he could get along. He made no comment as they skirted Graham's body. She didn't know whether he was taking anything in. It would be the blow to the head, she supposed. Together with the shock. He seemed to be concentrating on moving one foot in front of the other.

As they reached the first bend in the narrow path, she looked back. Simon was still standing there, staring out across the pool as if carved from stone.

★ ★ ★

The inquests and the funerals were behind them with the seasons and Dorothy's garden was blooming once more. Jen and Alan had returned to Sellybrook for the last time. Sunbeams were dancing in dust as they stood in the silent hallway.

Jen allowed her instincts to feel the atmosphere of the house and perhaps Alan was doing that too. She circled her arms round him and he responded, holding her close. She said, 'Are you all right?'

He was pressing his lips together, trying to smile. 'I think so. If you don't mind, I need to have some time to myself. I need to exorcise all the unpleasant parts of my childhood. And say goodbye. I'm not blocking you out, Jen, but it's something I have to do on my own.'

'I understand. And I won't be far away if you need me.' She went outside, concerned about Alan and forgetting to wonder whether she was all right herself. Every aspect of the house and garden was filled with memories. Here, waiting for the ambulance to arrive, she had told him about Graham and Dorothy and how his mother had died.

He had said, 'I know. I always knew. And so did Simon.'

'Graham said you knew. I wasn't sure whether I believed him.'

'I didn't allow myself to hear what he was telling me. We were back here, a while after she died, packing all the stuff away.' Alan had stopped, looking up at the house and she held on to him, her clothes dripping and wanting to check on Erica's drug-induced sleep but knowing how important it was to let him speak. Alan had been staring at nothing, looking into the screen of the past. And this scene too had played itself repeatedly in Jen's mind until she felt that she must have been there herself.

*   *   *

Alan was stacking their mother's books in boxes, trying not to think about what he was doing. They must find a tenant or sell as soon as they could. He didn't want it standing empty. A ghost house with nobody to decorate it at Christmas or weed Mum's garden.

Graham was edging from one foot to the other, not helping. 'Come on, Gray. You'll have to say if there's anything you want to keep.' Graham didn't answer. Alan stopped and looked at him. 'I know this is upsetting. It's the same for me. But it's happened. There's nothing we can do about it. Not now.' He knew that if only he had realised how bad his mother was feeling, there must have been actions he could have taken.

If he had only told her about his new idea in time, instead of dropping stupid hints. How she didn't have to part with the house altogether, she could rent it out and now he had a promotion, he would find a house in the south where there would be room for her too. She could have helped him choose. She would have enjoyed that. Or if she had needed help for her depression, he could have seen to that as well. All those missed opportunities.

Graham said, 'I wanted to talk to you, Alan. I made it all right, didn't I? You do see that. She was so unhappy, crying all the time.'

'I know. She tried to hide it from us.' Another shelf. Another row of once-loved book titles.

'Life held no future for her. I was here on my own and then I knew what to do. It was like Bobtail. I couldn't let her suffer. You do see?'

There was the rhythm of stacking and sorting, stacking and sorting and beyond that, Graham's voice going on and on and making no sense. And suddenly Alan did see. He slammed down the books he was holding and they scattered across the floor. He shouted, 'No. No. Anything but that. Don't tell me. I don't want to know.'

Rage and despair exploded inside his head and for the next few minutes he didn't know what was happening until he came back to himself and saw that Graham was lying on the floor crying and with blood on his face. He looked down at his fists. He said dully, 'Get out of here.'

Graham staggered to his feet. He opened his hands. 'I did what was best.'

'Go away.' Alan didn't want to talk about it or even think about it. And Graham was his brother. He couldn't even think of reporting him to the police. Dorothy wouldn't have wanted that.

From then on there was a new silence between them and Alan knew he must never, never bridge that silence. Alan coped with the terrible knowledge in the only way he could, by blocking it out. Making himself forget. Placing it into a secret part of his brain that he would refuse to access.

He didn't see his brother at all until he received the invitation to Graham and Lisa's wedding some years later. By then he could no longer understand his own reluctance and made himself attend. Even so, he maintained only a minimal contact with the couple. Perhaps that was why he had gone for Lisa, even though he disliked her. An eye for an eye, some kind of warped retaliation. He told Jen, 'I shouldn't have done any of that. I shouldn't have just left him to it. I should have made sure he got the psychiatric help he needed. But I must have been psychologically scarred myself. And I never dreamed he would be a danger to anyone else. And least of all, you.'

14

A few steps to the left and there was the herb garden and Jen remembered sitting there with Graham and that last long walk into the woodland. She didn't want to remember the pool. She took in a long slow breath. She had to confront it. If she did that, she might conquer her fear. If she didn't go now, she would always regret it. The pool would always be there, in her mind.

She went over to Dorothy's bank of golden flowers where the drive began and pulled out a handful of hypericum stems before turning to face the trees. Rose of Sharon. She stood for a moment and then took a step forward and the next was easier.

There was a figure on the path. She stopped again, hearing the rush of her own breath as she gasped. But it was only Simon Parkestone, his shabby green jacket blending with the leaves. She thrust the flowers into her pocket, not wanting to reveal her purpose for some reason she didn't understand herself.

He said, 'I saw the car. Is Alan about?'

She hesitated. 'He's busy at the moment but I don't expect he'll be long.'

He looked at his watch. 'It doesn't matter that much. Tell Alan I'm not worried about selling that land back to him now. I've done a deal on a leisure centre and clubhouse extension for the golf course and sold the original drive. We're making a new drive on that land behind your woods.'

It was too great a leap for her emotions to make. 'Oh, I see.' She tried to pull herself together. 'I suppose that will be easier.'

'Yes. When you come again, it will all look entirely different. And the new drive is what Dad always wanted to do and never got round to.'

'I don't think we will be coming again.'

'No.' He was nodding at her, as if coming to a decision. 'You OK?'

'Me? Oh, yes. Sorry. A bit preoccupied, that's all. This being the first time back here. It's not — easy.' And strange that Simon Parkestone was still standing here. He had given her the information to pass on and yet was showing no sign of leaving. It wasn't like him. Always so economical with words, abrupt to the edge of rudeness.

'And your mother? Erica?'

'Fine, thanks. Still gravely resenting having her stomach pumped because we'll never know whether it was necessary or not. She's convinced it wasn't.'

'I'm sure it was. Certain of it, in fact. It's the kind of thing Graham was capable of. And there is something else I'd like you to tell Alan.'

'Yes?'

'Graham blamed himself for Frank's death. He thought he had killed my

296

father. But he didn't, you know.'

'Yes, he told me. The chocolates. But it seems feasible. Whatever he gave to my mother was certainly very potent.'

'That's not what I meant. Graham didn't give Dad the chocolates. I did. I knew about them — or guessed. I took them in to Dad in the hospital knowing that.'

'You wanted to harm him?'

'I can't remember what I wanted. Or if I even knew at the time. It was obvious that Graham had tinkered with them when he gave them to me. It was a warning. His way of telling me to back off. I was angry with him for that — and I was always angry with my father. But Dad didn't eat them. He pushed the box in the locker though it would hardly fit and made some crack about expensive chocolates never making up for years of filial neglect. I was furious. But I didn't realise for a long time, how Graham had taken the guilt for Dad's death upon himself. Not until Graham came back here a couple of years ago.'

Recalling Graham's torment, Jen began to understand how the strange relationship had worked. 'But you didn't tell him?'

'No. That's how we were. Continually gaining points in an endless power struggle. Almost feeding off each other. Obsessed and obsessive.'

She said quietly, 'You would be relieved when it ended.'

He gave all his attention to his stick for a few minutes. 'No. Relief doesn't express my feelings. Not at all.'

She thought, guilt? And now was her only chance to talk about the cloud of grey guilt that was pressing her down, always at the back of her mind. 'Simon, I have to ask you. You dealt with the police and the inquest so — efficiently. I never thanked you. You made it look as if I hadn't killed Graham at all.' She held her breath. Now it was out in the open. Should she have spoken of it, even to Simon, who had been first on the scene? He could report her now

— and that was what she deserved. She should have owned up to it at the time. She had been in shock and the more she tried to get a firm grasp on what had happened, the more the memories slid away.

There was an odd look on his face. 'You didn't kill him.'

'But I did, I'm sure I did. I hit him with the stick, more than once.'

'I killed him.'

'What?' She took a step back.

'Or — let's say it's probable that I did. When we pulled him out of the water, you wanted to try artificial respiration, remember? I stopped you.'

'Yes, you did — but it was too late.'

He shook his head. 'Jen, he was still breathing. I knew it — and did nothing. I took a decision. I decided he had done enough damage. It was time I put things right. Because I had done nothing once before. I saw Graham coming away from the pool after killing his mother. When the news broke about Dorothy's death, I knew what he had done. And I did nothing.'

'But why?'

'I think you know. I was obsessed with Graham. I thought my knowledge would give me a hold over him and he would stay and never leave. But I released a monster who would kill again. So — when we pulled him out of the water, he was almost dead. What would reviving him achieve? What further harm would he do, even if he was imprisoned and eventually released? I waited, that's all.' His eyes were fixed on hers. His voice was firm and purposeful.

'I see.' She sighed. 'But — ' She stopped.

'Oh, I know. I shouldn't have taken the law into my own hands. I don't have the power of life and death. But neither did Graham. Hand me in, if you like, Jen. Phone the police. I shan't object.'

She hesitated. Unsure about the new suffering that would be unleashed. And for what?

'It makes little difference to me. I've

been punished. I'm living my punishment every day. When Graham came back here — well, I've never been so happy. We got along better than we ever had. I gave up any hope of ever regaining that when I neglected to save him. And I have to live on without him. You don't need to feel any guilt.'

She was remembering walking away from the pool, turning to see Simon standing over Graham. She said, 'But after I left — ' His expression stopped her.

His voice was little more than a whisper. 'Don't ask. Just be pleased that it's over. Get on with your life.' He smiled suddenly as if the conversation had never happened, and she could imagine what might have attracted Dorothy to his father. 'Well — give Alan my best.'

She stood with her hands in her coat pockets, looking after him and pitying his isolation. Trying to make sense of what he had told her. She didn't know how she felt about Simon's confession or what she would do. But the weight of the guilt that had burdened her since Graham's death was lifting. She had not been responsible. It wasn't her fault.

She heard footsteps on the gravel behind her and there was no time to go to the pool now because Alan was here. She looked into his face, trying to read his feelings and wondering whether he could read hers. 'Are you all right?'

He nodded, squeezing her shoulders. 'I think so. It's done me good to be quiet, where Mum used to be. But I've been wondering whether I could have done everything differently.'

'You can't blame yourself. Not for any of it. You were only twenty-one and you acted for the best, as you understood it at the time. None of us can ever do more than that. Come here.' She hugged him, clasping her arms round his back until she felt the taut muscles beginning to relax.

'What would I do without you? I'm much better now. I needed to come.'

He stood back. 'There's only one thing left to do. And you don't have to come if you don't want to.'

'You mean the pool? I do have to come. I do want to. I have to get that place out of my system.'

He sounded pleased. 'Me too. I'll just get the flowers. They're in the boot.'

'Flowers? When did you get those?'

He laughed. 'When I first went for petrol this morning.'

'Good idea. Why didn't I think of that?' No mention of Graham, she noted and perhaps they were both sounding too resolutely cheerful. But dealing with the flowers would get over the awkward moment. It would give them something to do.

They set off along the path. I will get through this, Jen thought. There wasn't room on the path to walk side by side. She kept her head down, aware only of Alan's back. When he stopped suddenly, she almost cannoned into him.

The pool was empty. They stared down at the drying mud and dead weed and tumbled rocks, saying nothing. Into the silence, they heard the distant machinery beginning a steady roar once more. Of course. She remembered Simon's original reason for seeking her out this afternoon. 'Those machines — they're working on Simon's new drive.'

'That's where the stream is,' Alan said. 'The source of the pool.'

'He said something about drainage.' She told him, briefly, what Simon had said about the work. 'Do you think he could have disturbed the incoming water source? Do you want to stop him? It may not be too late.'

The lines were seeping away from Alan's face. 'No. I think we're better without it. It seemed to cause nothing but misery.'

Yes. For Simon too, in the end. Fitting that he should have a hand in destroying it. She said, aware that her question seemed to have no connection, 'Did Graham really give Simon poisoned chocolates?'

She was surprised when he smiled. 'It was little more than a game then. He didn't like Simon, hated the way he always seemed to be hanging around. So he doctored a couple of orange creams and gave them to him and Simon was ill. Kept out of our hair for about a week. I knew about that and thought it was a laugh, harmless. I didn't know about the whole box. Not until later. Much later. I should have taken it more seriously but he was only a kid. And so was I.'

'And that led to Graham thinking he was the cause of Frank's death and also his mother's misery.' Jen was nodding, organising the information and adding these last pieces of the puzzle.

'Yes. Graham and I did a lot of things together. The plant collection was my idea in the first place. One of my enthusiasms and Graham tagged along, like he usually did. But when I got fed up and went on to making tree houses or something, he stuck with it. And began to concentrate on herbs.' Jen was going to tell him, once more, that he mustn't blame himself, but he was smiling now. 'We were often happy, you know, as kids. Dad didn't ruin everything.'

'Of course not. You can hang on to the good bits.'

'I will. And this can be a new start for you and me. All the depression and tragedy of the past has drained away with the water. We can put it all behind us and move on.' He put his arm round her. 'I could never have gotten through this without you.'

There had been so many times when Jen had felt helpless, certain she was making mistakes and taking events in all kinds of wrong directions. 'I could have made better judgements. Some of my actions were rooted in fear.' She took a breath. 'Particularly in everything to do with Maria.' It was still difficult to mention Maria. Jen supposed it always would be.

'I know. It's OK. Forget Maria. I broke it off with her because she was so ruthless, even then. She wanted to sell the house too — while telling Mum the exact opposite.'

Jen must speak, otherwise she might never find the courage again. 'Maria heightened all my insecurities. I've always felt I was trudging along behind you. When your mind takes off on some new flight path I can't always open wings of inspiration and dance up there with you.'

'Oh, Jen. No.' His lips brushed her cheek. 'You give me something to hold on to. You help me keep my feet on the ground. I need you so much. Without you, I'd be floating off into the ether like a lost helium balloon.' He grinned as she laughed out loud. 'Don't ever stop laughing at me, Jen.'

'I won't.' They stood together in silence. A shadow crossed Alan's face. 'When I thought I'd lost you, I've never been so terrified. Graham came running up to me and said you'd had an accident by the pool. I knew I couldn't bear it happening again. Not to you, Jen. Not you.'

She said, 'Ssh. I'm here.'

'I know. When I came round and saw your face, leaning over me . . . The relief brought a pain of its own. Like a vivid migraine headache. And that was when I remembered for the first time. I remembered everything I'd blocked out and kept hidden.' He put one hand across his eyes. 'And I was responsible for putting you in terrible danger. I couldn't live without you, Jen. You've made me whole. For the first time, I'd allowed myself to stop running. I needed to make time for our love, slowly but surely.'

And Jen had stupidly misunderstood. Locked in her own fears, she had felt she could never keep up with him, whereas he hadn't wanted someone to keep up. His need was to stop and learn how to become himself. You couldn't keep running forever. 'We make a good whole. I love you, Alan.' Sometimes she couldn't believe how much she loved him.

Alan pushed the flower stems down

into the damp earth at the head of the natural basin where the water had seeped in. A swift breeze took a handful of golden petals and strewed them across the black mud.

Jen's fingers found the hypericum stems from Dorothy's garden she had pushed into her pocket. She brought them out and threw them down too. For Dorothy, she thought, and Frank. For Lisa and Maria. Black and gold. Light and dark. And for Graham.

We do hope that you have enjoyed reading this large print book.

Did you know that all of our titles are available for purchase?

We publish a wide range of high quality large print books including:
**Romances, Mysteries, Classics
General Fiction
Non Fiction and Westerns**

Special interest titles available in large print are:
**The Little Oxford Dictionary
Music Book, Song Book
Hymn Book, Service Book**

Also available from us courtesy of Oxford University Press:
**Young Readers' Dictionary
(large print edition)
Young Readers' Thesaurus
(large print edition)**

For further information or a free brochure, please contact us at:
**Ulverscroft Large Print Books Ltd.,
The Green, Bradgate Road, Anstey,
Leicester, LE7 7FU, England.
Tel:** (00 44) 0116 236 4325
Fax: (00 44) 0116 234 0205

Other titles in the
Linford Romance Library:

GIRL WITH A GOLD WING

Jill Barry

It's the 1960s, and Cora Murray dreams of taking to the skies — so when her father shows her a recruitment advertisement for air hostesses, she jumps at the chance to apply. Passing the interview with flying colours, she throws herself into her training, where she is quite literally swept off her feet by First Officer Ross Anderson. But whilst Ross is charming and flirtatious, he's also engaged — and Cora's former boyfriend Dave is intent on regaining her affections . . .

THE SURGEON'S MISTAKE

Chrissie Loveday

Matti Harper has been in love with Ian Faulkner since their school days. He is now an eminent cardiac surgeon, she his theatre nurse. Ian has finally fallen in love — the trouble is, it's with Matti's flatmate Lori! But whilst a heartbroken Matti prepares to be their bridesmaid, Lori is being suspiciously flirtatious with another man. How can Matti tell Ian without appearing to be jealous? Best man Sam Grayling tries to help, but only succeeds in sending things from bad to worse . . .